Sara longs for a new life.

Sara rummaged through her travel bag and withdrew a miniature looking glass. Yesterday the bruise on her jaw had been a ghastly shade of yellow but it had faded, and today it was hardly noticeable.

Her eyes met their reflection and she recognized a flicker of apprehension. She drew a deep breath and forced her muscles to relax. This was going to work out fine. It had to.

Gazing out the window through beads of water, she watched the landscape sweep by. All her hopes rested in the faith that Mr. McClain was a decent man and that this marriage, although unorthodox, would prove satisfactory.

Oh, how she wanted a new life! To be happy and free, away from the oppression of her stepfather. To be at peace in her own home.

DENISE HUNTER lives in Indiana with her husband and three active, young sons. As the only female of the household, every day is a new adventure, but Denise holds on to the belief that her most important responsibility in this life is to raise her children in such a way that they will love and fear the Lord. *Stranger's Bride* is her first published novel. The message Denise wants her writing to convey is that "God needs to be the center of our lives. If He isn't, everything else is out of kilter."

Stranger's Bride

Denise Hunter

Heartsong Presents

Lovingly dedicated to my husband Kevin, who believed in me long before I did. Your encouragement and support are a gift from God. Also, in memory of my grandfather, John David Waters, whose faithfulness left a legacy of blessings to the generations to follow. Finally, to my Lord and Savior, who never gives up on me!

A note from the author:
I love to hear from my readers! You may correspond with me by writing: **Denise Hunter**
Author Relations
PO Box 719
Uhrichsville, OH 44683

ISBN 1-57748-553-X

STRANGER'S BRIDE

Cover illustration by Victoria Lisi and Julius.

PRINTED IN THE U.S.A.

one

1887

Sara Donaldson hunkered down low on the cellar steps. Above her shone a ribbon of light where the cellar door met the kitchen floor. Normally, a rug concealed the entrance, but now it was slightly askew after Sara's rush into the dark hiding place.

"Sara!"

The shout, accompanied by the slam of the door, caused Sara to jump, and she bumped her head on the wooden door. A hand flew to cover her mouth.

"Sara, where are you, brat?" he slurred.

The sound of his heavy boots as he ascended the stairs to the second floor caused Sara to go limp. Perhaps when he didn't find her in her room he would collapse on his bed.

She clutched the bulky traveling bag to her stomach and settled back to wait, hoping she wouldn't miss her train. If she hadn't been waylaid on the way home from work by that pitiful dog, she'd be well on her way to the depot instead of being trapped in the damp cellar.

She shivered and snuggled deeper into her tattered overcoat. After her mother died, Sara had become the target of Pete's rampages. She winced with the memory of her mother's beatings. She knew she would never forget the sounds she'd heard from the sanctuary of her room—the gruesome sound of flesh pummeling flesh.

Her mother had worn the evidence of Pete's brutality

5

like a badge of survival. The puffy discolorations on her face and body never had time to heal completely. Just as Sara had started to see some semblance of her mother's natural face, he'd repeat his brutal assault.

Some nights he would come home sober now, and others he would come home wild and ruthless. Last night had been the latter, and Sara's jaw smarted from the blow she'd received.

The edge of the wooden step dug into her thigh and she quietly shifted her weight to alleviate the discomfort. The rustling of paper reminded her of the envelope in her pocket. She slipped her hand into the cavity and curled her fingers around the well-worn paper.

Three months ago her best friend, Helen, had shown her the advertisement from the *Boston Herald*. "I thought you might find this interesting," Helen had said. The ad read:

WANTED: WIFE
Desire good Christian woman, age 21–28, to marry Kansas rancher. Must be willing to live away from city. Send letter of interest to:
Nathan McClain
McClain Ranch
Cedar Springs, Kansas

"You can't be serious! I don't know anything about this man. Aside from that, I'm only nineteen, as you well know. Anyway, he wants a religious woman."

After Helen left the room, Sara had tucked the ad into her pinafore to reread later. She wasn't an impetuous young woman, and what had made her save that ad, she didn't know. But on that day the thought was planted in her head, and it took root like a seedling in rich soil.

The thumping of heavy footsteps jerked Sara's mind to the present. Her heart rate accelerated, and she parted her lips to quiet her breathing. Pete could be like a panther when he was stalking someone. He'd found her more than once, and she'd paid for her evasiveness.

He reached the bottom of the stairs. His footsteps paused for a moment, then grew louder.

"Sara!"

The floor above her groaned. She instinctively sank lower, wishing she could somehow melt into the grungy floor beneath her.

The step she huddled on creaked under her weight. The sound seemed to echo through the darkness. She squeezed her eyes shut and held her breath. The footsteps scraped to a halt directly overhead. *Please, oh, please. . .*

The door above was flung open and light shattered her damp hiding place. Sara's scream caught in her throat.

"You worthless piece of garbage! How dare you hide from me!"

He grabbed the collar of her dress and hauled her up from the depths of the cellar like a wet kitten held by the scruff of its neck. The neck band tightened painfully around her throat and her bag fell to the floor with a thud. Her fingers pulled at the choking material, but she got relief only when Pete flung her across the table.

A muffled sob escaped as she hit the floor, landing on her right leg. She gasped for breath and looked up to see the murderous expression on Pete's face. He moved toward her.

Gathering her feet under her, Sara scooted backward, a futile effort that placed her against the wall behind her. Not for the first time, she pleaded. "Please. . .I didn't. . .I was only. . ."

Pete stopped. Sara stared in confusion as he raised a

hand to his head. He started to speak, then closed his mouth. His whole body wavered like a timbering tree. He shook his head, as if trying to clear it, and blinked several times in rapid succession. Sara watched, her breath caught in her throat. Pete took one final step forward before collapsing, taking a rickety chair down with him. His head hit the floor with a thump, only inches from her feet.

Sara sat, immobile. His eyes were closed, and he breathed shallowly through his gaping mouth, emitting fetid puffs of breath.

She cautiously slid up the wall. Stepping around his massive body, she grabbed her bag, then scrambled across the room. The room passed in a blur, and Sara made no effort to be quiet as she threw the door open, letting it bang against the wall.

Without delay she dashed over the threshold and scurried down the wet street, sloshing through puddles in her rush. Her pale yellow dress billowed out behind her as she disappeared into the fray of wagons and pedestrians.

two

Nathan McClain had just finished rubbing down the black stallion when the heavens opened up and shot volleys of cold water into the dry dirt. He'd known it was coming, had smelled the promised rain in the air, and was grateful to be in the barn for the moment.

He led Thunder to his stall, shut the gate, and shoved his worn black hat on his head. He bounded the fifty yards to the farmhouse, his hat little protection from the deluge, then vaulted up the wooden steps, two at a time, to the wraparound porch. After removing his hat and boots, he stepped into the house and was greeted by the aroma of Hetty's mouthwatering pot roast.

"Nathan, is that you?"

"Yeah, Hetty. Sorry I'm late." He padded into the kitchen.

Hetty's husband, Gus, shoveled a heaping spoon of potatoes into his mouth. "You'd best get to eatin' if you want me to save you any."

Hetty snapped a towel at Gus. "Never you mind this husband of mine. There's plenty for the three of us, with leftovers, too. Why don't you scoot upstairs and get yourself into some dry clothes? I'm keepin' a plate warm for you."

"Think I might just do that."

Minutes later Nathan reappeared, wearing cotton trousers and a blue plaid shirt. Hetty removed his plate from the top of the stove and set it in front of him as he seated himself at the head of the table.

"Did you take Thunder out for some exercise?" Gus

pushed his plate away and leaned back in the sturdy oak chair.

"Yeah, that's why I was late."

"Listen to that," said Gus, referring to the rain pattering on the roof. "Looks like spring has finally arrived."

"Not a moment too soon for me," Hetty said. "You know how anxious I am to get those vegetables planted. There's nothin' like puttin' seeds in the earth and lettin' God grow us some tasty food."

"Don't get too anxious now, darlin'. We may be in for some late frost this year. Weather's been mighty cold for April."

"Don't I know it! It's been messin' with my garden plans! Why, if it doesn't warm up soon, our crops won't be in before cold sets in again!"

When Nathan finished his food, Hetty cleared the dishes and hung the towel to dry.

Gus rose from the table and went to collect his hat. "You 'bout ready, darlin'? This old man is tired tonight."

"Oh, Gus, you're only forty-nine. Besides, you've got more pep than most twenty-year-olds." Hetty joined him at the door.

Gus laughed and looked pointedly at Nathan. "You see there, Nathan? That's why you need a wife. Keeps you thinkin' you're young!"

"Now hush up, Gus. That boy don't need no advice from you."

Once they'd gone to their cabin, Nathan stoked the fire, then lowered his body into the tan, fabric-covered chair, his considerable weight causing it to groan in protest. His black shoulder-length hair was still damp on the ends where his hat had not covered it. The house was silent, except for the crackling of the fire, punctuated by an occasional snap.

Nathan settled back in the chair and let himself reflect on the last ten months. It was hard to believe Pop had been gone that long. The night he'd died had been the saddest of Nathan's life, but he couldn't help being relieved that Pop's suffering was over.

He was in a better place now—probably griping to his wife about what a stubborn boy she'd left him to raise alone. The corner of Nathan's mouth rose as he pictured his wiry pop laying into the mother Nathan had never known. She'd been a sturdy woman, judging by the portrait that hung over the fireplace. Her wavy brown hair had been worn up, and she'd had green eyes; Pop had said they were greener than grass in the springtime. Nathan had never known her, though. Never grieved for her the way he'd grieved for Pop.

The pain he'd felt at his father's passing had soon turned to hurt and anger when an attorney named VanCleeves, from Wichita, appeared on his doorstep just three days after Pop's death.

His father, Mr. VanCleeves informed him, had hired him to draw up a will at the beginning of his illness. Nathan accepted the envelope Mr. VanCleeves drew from his suit coat pocket, and read it. The wording was complex— almost foreign—to Nathan.

He regarded Mr. VanCleeves with a blank look and shook his head. "I'm sorry, but I'm afraid the meaning just isn't sinking in."

"Quite all right, Mr. McClain; I'm happy to explain. As you know, your father held the deed to the McClain Ranch, which his father had passed on to him." Nathan nodded and Mr. VanCleeves continued. "Naturally, your father wanted to pass the ranch on to you, you being his only child and all. He knew that this ranch has been your life ever since you were old enough to sit in a saddle. He was worried that you would go through life dedicated solely to running the ranch."

Nathan's brows drew together. "What are you getting at, Mr. VanCleeves?"

"Let me speak plainly to you, Mr. McClain. Your father confided in me that he felt if things were left as they are, you might never marry and start a family of your own. He didn't see interest on your part in your settling down and taking a wife. Of course, he realized there are few marriage-able young women in the area. But still, more than any-thing, he desired to see you happily married, with a lovely woman and children to call your own. I'm sure you're aware of the deep love your father had for your mother. You see, Mr. McClain, he wanted that for you as well."

"I know all this, Mr. VanCleeves. My father was always trying to persuade me to take someone to a church social or a picnic, and I would do it. Still do sometimes. But I have no desire to marry. I just can't see myself settling down with a woman, and my father knew that. I'm content with my life here on the ranch. It's what I know. . .what I love."

"I'm glad we're getting back to the ranch, Son, because that's what the will is all about. It states, as per your father's wishes, that you will inherit the deed to the McClain Ranch immediately. However, if after twelve months from your father's death you are not yet married, the ranch is to be sold. You will, of course, be entitled to all proceeds from the—"

"Sold! He couldn't have done that! This ranch has been in our family for three generations. Why would he force me into a marriage I don't want?" A relieving thought burst into his mind. "There's a way out of this, right? A man can't be forced to marry. My father's gone now. What difference could it possibly make if I were just given the deed?"

"Technically, Mr. McClain, you're not being forced to marry. You may instead sell the ranch after twelve months' time. As for the document itself, I'm afraid it's a perfectly legal will and I'm bound by law to see that its provisions are carried out to the letter."

Nathan sank into the nearest chair and ran a hand through his hair.

"I'm sorry to deliver this shock to you. I can see you need some time to adjust to the news. If you have any questions, feel free to contact me at my office in Wichita. The address is on the document."

Mr. VanCleeves saw himself out, and Nathan sat in the chair for what seemed like hours.

The next two months passed in a blur, and he found himself caught in a maelstrom of emotions, grieving one moment, angry the next. A haze of confusion enveloped him as he struggled to understand the reasoning behind his father's strange will. It was easier to dwell on his emotions than face the decisions he knew he had to make.

Nathan shared the news with no one; those around him attributed his moodiness to his father's death. Even Hetty left him alone to his thoughts. Not that he could blame her. He'd been as cranky as an old grizzly.

Six months had passed by the time he reached a decision. Marriage, unappealing as it sounded, was better than losing the ranch.

That decided, he considered whom to ask. Laura Reed was nice enough, and he'd known her most of his life, but it really wouldn't be fair to her. She deserved a normal marriage with a husband who loved her. And she was more like a sister to him than a wife. Besides, Mrs. Reed would be an unbearable mother-in-law.

He'd courted other young ladies but most of them were married now. And the others—well, he just couldn't picture it. Mara Lawton was new to town and she'd practically thrown herself at him, but he'd heard about her cruel rejection of Daniel Parnell and had concluded that she was a bit too snooty for his liking.

He didn't know where the idea came from. One minute he was saddling up Starbuck, the next he was planning what the advertisement would say. After he prayed about it, he listed it in the *Boston Herald* and waited to see what the response would be.

About a week after the advertisement appeared, there were three letters from Boston waiting for him at the post office. The next day there were two. They flowed in steadily for about a week. He had no idea so many young ladies would want to marry a Kansas rancher. It could make a man heady to think so many women would have him. Except they didn't know him from Adam. If Mrs. Leighton at the post office noticed the sudden spurt of letters—all from Boston—she didn't say anything. At least not to him.

The fourth letter he received was from a Miss Sara Donaldson. He knew when he read it that she was the one. She described herself as five feet three inches tall, slim, dark-haired, and twenty-one years old. She desired to start a new life out West, away from the city. What appealed to him most about the letter was its tone. The others ran the gamut from gushy to downright prissy, but Miss Donaldson's sounded sensible and matter-of-fact. Almost detached. This was what he wanted. A wife, yet not really. She didn't sound like someone given to teary episodes or hurt feelings, someone he'd have to tiptoe around all the time. She was probably plain-looking—who else would choose a husband from an ad?—but that didn't matter so much to him. In fact, he preferred it. That would make it easy for him to maintain a distance. No need to go getting involved with her.

He waited until the letters began to taper off, then wrote a letter telling Miss Donaldson that he'd been impressed with her letter and would appreciate it if she would meet him in Wichita in late April. He assured her the train fare would be taken care of and asked that she write and let him know if this was agreeable—and if it was, when she would arrive.

He received her reply shortly after he sent his letter. She would arrive in Wichita April 26, on the 6:00 train.

The flames slowly came into focus as his thoughts returned to the present. Three days away and he hadn't even told Hetty and Gus. He'd tell them tomorrow. Not the whole story, but at least the part about Miss Donaldson and his ad. There was no telling how they'd react. In fact, there was no telling how the town of Cedar Springs would react.

three

The blaring whistle of the steam locomotive startled Sara awake. She reached into her pocket. The timepiece she kept there read 8:00. Sara yawned. She would be glad to get into a genuine bed and sleep peacefully for an entire night.

Her thoughts carried her in another direction; tonight she would meet the man who would be her husband.

Helen had had her best interests at heart when she showed Sara that ad. Only Helen knew the truth of Sara's circumstances. Only Helen cared enough to help her find a way out.

It was her dear friend who had helped her compose her first letter to Mr. McClain. The contents of it made her a little uneasy even now. His advertisement had requested a Christian woman, and while she wasn't particularly religious, she did have a Bible, and she considered herself to be a good person. She'd also written that she was twenty-one years old—a fifteen-month exaggeration—since he'd requested an older woman. Other than that, she'd been completely honest, although she had omitted the details concerning her desire to leave Boston. There was no need to give him any ideas, after all.

It hadn't seemed real until she had received his letter of acceptance. Helen had been with her when she'd gotten the letter from the post office. They'd sat right on the dusty steps of the old building and read it together, her hands trembling with anticipation.

Helen had pulled Sara up and spun her around in a victory dance after reading the first paragraph. It had all seemed so right at that moment. Helen was sure and brave enough for the both of them. It was only later, as she lay alone in bed that night, that she began to wonder if it was all a horrible mistake.

The only real information she had about Mr. McClain was that he was a Christian, twenty-nine years old, owned a ranch in Kansas, and had advertised for a wife in the newspaper. What sort of man did that? His letter sounded rather impersonal, which was fine, but left her wondering about his character. Did he treat others fairly? Was he a gentleman? Did he have a temper? Worse yet, was he a drinker?

Her present situation was onerous, but she was treading into unfamiliar territory. What if Mr. McClain were worse than Pete? She didn't share her concerns with Helen, who seemed so optimistic. And every time Sara started to bring it up, she wound up feeling like she must be seeing trouble where there was none.

For two days she weighed her options. She could go to Kansas and take her chances with Mr. McClain or she could stay here and continue saving and working toward her own independence. Given her meager earnings from the Hotel Vendôme, it would take at least another year to put away enough money. Perhaps she was impatient, but another year of living with Pete seemed like eternity. He was becoming progressively more violent and coming home drunk more than ever before.

While she didn't know much about Mr. McClain, he was a religious man, and that should count for something. To live far away in Cedar Springs, Kansas had its appeal as well. The town's name itself conjured up lovely scenes of giant trees and gushing water. Sometimes the unknown simply is more attractive than the familiar; perhaps that was why she decided to accept Mr. McClain's proposal.

Leaving her friend was her only regret. She knew it would be risky to remain in contact with Helen. Pete knew they were friends, and Sara only hoped that he wouldn't harass Helen once he discovered Sara missing. Sara was glad Helen had her brother for protection, even though Helen insisted she was not intimidated by "that old drunk," as she called Pete.

Sara had not even given advance notice to her employer for fear that Pete would find out she was quitting her job. Mr. Stalfort had not taken her short notice kindly. He had pursed his thin lips as he wrote out her final paycheck, subtracting two days pay for the inconvenience of her late notice.

Ever since she'd finally made it to the train, Sara had been worrying about what Mr. McClain would think of *her*. What if he didn't like her? What if he found her unsightly? Pete had always called her scrawny and said her thick curls were unruly and brazen. He'd called her names, too. Many of them were unfamiliar, but she could tell by his scathing tone and malicious expression that they were horrible.

Sara rummaged through her travel bag and withdrew a miniature looking glass. Yesterday the bruise on her jaw had been a ghastly shade of yellow but it had faded, and today it was hardly noticeable.

Her eyes met their reflection and she recognized a flicker of apprehension. She drew a deep breath and forced her muscles to relax. This was going to work out fine. It had to.

Gazing out the window through beads of water, she

watched the landscape sweep by. All her hopes rested in
the faith that Mr. McClain was a decent man and that this
marriage, although unorthodox, would prove satisfactory.

Oh, how she wanted a new life! To be happy and free,
away from the oppression of her stepfather. To be at peace
in her own home.

She so wanted to do this right. Pete had always made her
nervous. It seemed as if he were forever waiting for her to
make a mistake. And he never had long to wait. It was
easy to burn supper or miss a speck of dirt when Pete was
growling at you from across the room. It had taken these
long days of travel for her nerves to settle from the constant tension of living with Pete.

The tall trees beside the train track sailed by like grand
ships being driven by a mighty wind. It was a dismal day
outside. The sky was a gray abyss, hiding all evidence of
yesterday's sun. Nevertheless, she enjoyed the countryside
as it rolled by. It was a splendid change from Boston's
landscape. She was ready for a quieter life.

Sara wondered how far Mr. McClain lived from Wichita.
It didn't matter. She was looking forward to the solitude.
Not that they would be alone. He'd mentioned in his last
letter that his ranch hand, Gus, lived in another house on
the property with his wife, Hetty. They were to be the wit-
nesses at the wedding tomorrow.

She leaned her head against the cool window and
attempted to recapture some much-needed sleep.

When she awoke, she saw that a young girl occupied the
seat next to her. Most of the morning and afternoon were
spent listening to her chatter. Abbey was traveling to Texas
to visit her grandmother. When Abbey asked Sara who
she was going to visit, Sara simply said she was going
home. Sara wasn't accustomed to such a lively person, but

Abbey was delightful and amusing, and she helped to pass the day.

When the next stop was Wichita, Sara smoothed the creases in her deep blue dress. She wished she had something more becoming to wear today. Her nicest dress, an ivory gown trimmed with a flounce and sporting a bustle, was being saved for tomorrow. Her mama had sewn it several years ago, and it was a bit out of fashion; still, it was her fanciest dress. Anyway, it would feel nice to wear something her mama had made; it would be almost like having her there for her wedding. For today, her blue frock would have to do. Besides, that's what she'd told Mr. McClain she'd be wearing. The matching blue ribbon in her hair would further serve to identify her.

When the Wichita stop was announced, Sara stood and gathered her belongings. Abbey rose to let her by, and after a quick embrace, they bid each other farewell.

The train was a little early, and as she disembarked she wondered if Mr. McClain had even arrived yet. The Wichita stop was a popular one, judging by the number of people who disembarked with her.

Once her feet were on the wooden platform, she cast a furtive glance around. There were several groups of people greeting loved ones, but she saw no one matching Mr. McClain's description. She shifted her weight awkwardly for a moment, then lugged her case to a vacant bench against the wall of the depot, and perched on the edge of the bench to wait.

Her mama had used the expression "bundle of nerves" often, and it came to mind now as she sat waiting for her husband-to-be. Every part of her body seemed to be affected. Her cold hands were trembling, her legs felt like noodles, her heart was beating out a cadence to a speedy tune, and her thoughts were ricocheting from one side of her head to the other.

She glanced up each time she heard the tromping of feet on the hollow landing, but no one seemed to be looking for her as they shuffled by. The crowd was clearing, the new boarders having gotten on, and only their family members stood on the platform now, waiting to wave good-bye.

According to her timepiece it was still a few minutes before 6:00, so she scooted back on the rugged bench and waited for her future to materialize.

≥

Hetty's excitement was obvious in the way she fidgeted all the way to Wichita. She clearly was looking forward to having another Christian woman around the house.

As for Nathan, he just wanted to get this farce of a wedding behind him and get on with his life. This woman's presence in his life would be an inconvenience, but he felt things could pretty much go on as they always had.

They'd heard the shrill whistle of the train as Nathan pulled the carriage to a stop. Gus and Hetty insisted Nathan meet Miss Donaldson alone, so he tethered the horses and hurried off to find her.

Several people lingered in the train station, some saying hello, some saying good-bye, but there was no young lady fitting Miss Donaldson's description.

He went to the rear of the building, stepped out onto the platform, and scanned the area. He saw a few people milling about before his eyes settled on her. She was sitting on a bench no more than fifteen feet away. A blue dress hung upon her frame, and he could see from her profile the blue ribbon secured in her upswept hair. Stubborn ringlets of dark satin had escaped and teased her face as a

gentle breeze blew. Her eyes were cast downward, studying her little black boots, and her hands were folded
demurely in her lap. Even from a distance he could see her
smooth ivory skin and delicately rounded nose.

His jaw hardened and his eyes narrowed as he studied
her. This wasn't the homely young woman he'd imagined,
the one he'd been planning to disregard, the one who was
simply supposed to share his house and whose presence he
would scarcely heed.

He couldn't ignore this woman, pretend she wasn't
there.

He felt betrayed, as if she'd deceived him; she had made
him believe she was uncomely, when, in fact, she was
exquisite!

With time he would have seen the absurdity of these
thoughts. But as he stomped over to where she sat, anger
boiled up within him, threatening to spew out.

Sara heard the heavy footsteps coming toward her and
knew instinctively who it was. She kept her eyes trained
on her boots and bit her trembling lip.

Massive black boots scuffed to a halt several feet away.
Her eyes followed the long line of his legs and torso. He
was a big, strapping man, even taller than her stepfather.
Corded muscles bulged below his rolled cuffs, and his
neck extended columnlike from beneath his collar.

His jaw was angular and tight, his lips compressed in a
firm line, and the brows over his gray eyes were drawn
low, causing two vertical creases between them.

He might have been handsome, if not for the scowl on his
face. She wondered what she'd done to provoke this man.

She levered her body off the bench, forcing her quaking
legs to support her weight.

He removed his worn hat, exposing hair the color of coal

hanging in waves to his shoulders. "Miss Donaldson?" he asked between clenched teeth.

"Y–yes," she said, wishing she were anyone else.

"I'm Nathan McClain." He reluctantly offered his hand.

Sara timidly extended her own and found it swallowed up in a brusque handshake. "It. . .it's a pleasure to meet you, Mr. McClain." It came out in a croak, but he didn't seem to notice.

"Hope you haven't been waiting too long," he continued before she could answer. "This all you brought with you?"

"Uh, yes, j–just the one bag."

He picked up the valise as if it weighed no more than a dishcloth. "We'd best be going. Hetty and Gus are waiting in the carriage."

Sara walked briskly behind him, trying to keep pace with his long strides. Through the depot and down the steps they went. All the while, her mind was racing as fast as her feet. *What have I done? How can I marry this man?* Questions surged through her in waves, churning up doubts and eroding her peace of mind.

four

There was no time to challenge her sanity or sort through her options, as she soon found herself standing beside an old carriage that held a middle-aged couple.

The woman, Hetty, was plump, with brown hair that was turning gray on the sides. Sara's face relaxed in a small smile as Hetty beamed at her, then leaned over the carriage to catch hold of Sara's hand. "You must be Sara. Oh, you are a dear! But you must be exhausted after that dreadful long ride."

Gus bounded down from the carriage and politely extended a hand. "Pleasure to meet you, miss. Let me give you a hand up." He was a little on the thin side, his hair speckled with gray, but his face sported a welcoming grin.

Sara mounted the carriage in front of Hetty, and Mr. McClain vaulted up on the opposite side. The seat was plenty wide for two people, but he was such a large man that Sara had to wedge herself against the bench's arm to keep from touching him. He snapped the reins, setting the team in motion, and said nothing.

Hetty filled the silence with friendly chatter. "I think you'll find Wichita much like Boston, Sara. When me and Gus came here eleven years ago, there wasn't a train station or nothin'. Now I hear tell there's forty thousand people livin' in the area. And just look at those buildings! Four stories high, some of 'em, and made of brick."

The dirt road—Douglas Street, the sign read—was lined on both sides by various-sized buildings. People carrying

24

packages or toting children scurried by on the street-side paths. Horse-drawn wagons clattered by with heavy loads. The city did, indeed, bear a resemblance to Boston.

Hetty explained that they would be staying at a local hotel. She asked if Sara had eaten yet, and when Sara said she hadn't, Gus told her they'd have supper in the hotel dining room.

Mr. McClain had remained silent all the while, and Sara dared a peek at him through a fringe of lashes. His rigid body scarcely swayed with the carriage's movement, and his large hands gripped the reins so tightly his knuckles had gone white. Her eyes skittered up to his face and she saw that it was still dark with anger.

Since he'd been fuming before she'd even spoken, she reached the only conclusion she could possibly draw: He was displeased with her appearance. Well, she'd feared this would happen. Had expected it, really. Her appearance surely did seem to incite men to anger. First Pete, now Mr. McClain.

He probably wouldn't want to marry her at all now, and perhaps that was for the best. She wasn't keen on living with another ill-tempered man. Mercy, but she did bring out the worst in men.

Reality haunted her and she remembered her paltry savings. At best it would buy her two night's lodging, and it was doubtful she'd be able to secure employment without a letter of recommendation. One thing she was certain of: Mr. Stalfort would not send her a letter of recommendation even if she begged for it. Oh, why hadn't she thought this through? At the very least she should have stalled for time to save a bit more money. Now she had no options open to her. What had she been thinking?

If Mr. McClain chose not to marry her, he might offer to

pay her fare back to Boston, but she had no desire to go back there. Mr. Stalfort would certainly not rehire her, and Pete would surely find her if she were anywhere in Boston. Helen would probably offer to take her in once again, but she refused to bring trouble upon her friend's household. And where else could she go? There were no distant relatives who might take pity on her, even if she were willing to take charity.

All she could do was hope that Mr. McClain hadn't changed his mind. She would follow through with her plan and make the best of it. Perhaps he wasn't such a wretched man after all. People were entitled to have bad days now and then. Besides, he couldn't be that awful and have such warm and congenial friends.

She peeked at him again and, observing no change in his demeanor, she resolved to try to please him in any way she could. Even if her appearance disappointed him, there were other ways she could please him. She knew how to take care of a house, had been doing it since her mother had died. And even Mr. Stalfort had no complaint with her cleaning.

The carriage drew to a halt at the hotel. Gus assisted Sara and Hetty, while Nathan looped the reins around the hitching post.

Once inside, a chambermaid showed them to their rooms. Hetty suggested they freshen up and meet in the dining room in fifteen minutes. Sara agreed, eager for a moment alone and wanting to splash some cold water on her face. Thankfully, Nathan had requested three rooms, which meant Sara would have the whole night to gather her courage for tomorrow. And she had a notion it would take her the whole night.

As she entered the room, she noted that the hotel was

more civilized than she'd expected to find in the West. Not lavish, like the Hotel Vendôme, but stylish and clean.

She doused her face with water from the basin and peered in the looking glass as she blotted her face dry. Her hair looked a fright, so she let it down and combed out the snarls. That done, she swept it up again in an effort to tame the thick mane of curls.

Next, she withdrew her wedding dress from the valise and hung it on a peg. There were some creases in the delicate material, but she supposed they would fall out. She looked at the dress and remembered the hours her mama had spent on it. *Oh, Mama, I miss you so!*

Besides the ivory gown, she had only the dress on her back and one other, a calico, soft from wear. The other items in her bag—toiletries, a nightie, underclothes, an old Bible, and her mother's picture—would be enough to see her through. It wasn't much, but she hadn't wanted to be encumbered by a larger bag.

She saw by her timepiece that only two minutes remained until their appointed meeting time, so she checked her appearance one more time and hastened to the dining room.

As she descended the stairs, she saw the threesome sitting at a circular table near the center of the room. Once again she was surprised by the refinement of this western town. White linen cloths covered tables that were set with china and surrounded by wooden, spindled chairs. Shaded lanterns, elegantly suspended by three cords, hung overhead. Shades were drawn halfway on the west side of the room in an effort to block the glare of the setting sun.

Though the dining room was only half full, the room was alive with the clanking of sterling on china and the buzz of idle chatter. Fried chicken was the prominent aroma, and the smell prompted a growl from Sara's empty stomach as she made her way to the table. She'd had no appetite for days, but she would eat well tonight, if only to stop the knawing in her stomach.

Nathan was speaking to Gus and Hetty as Sara approached the table, and for the first time she saw his face at ease. She realized her earlier assessment was correct; Mr. McClain was a fine-looking man.

Sara took her seat, and the steady stream of conversation came to an abrupt halt as Mr. McClain became aware of her presence. His face closed and he once again became the daunting image she remembered.

Smiling broadly, Hetty solicitously filled the gap. "Hello again, Sara. I hope you found the room to your liking."

"Yes, it's lovely," she said softly.

Hetty gave her linen napkin a flip and arranged it on her lap. "We've been here before and we recommend the fried chicken, if you've a liking for it. The dumplin's are good, too, although not as tasty as mine, if I do say so!"

"Amen to that, darlin'. This here's the finest cook in the West, Sara. Look here; I got the waistline to prove it!"

Hetty rapped him on the shoulder. "Gus, you don't have a spare inch on that bony body of yours, and if that's a reflection on my cookin', I reckon I'm failin' miserable!"

Sara smiled as she watched the bantering between the couple. She let her eyes skitter over to Mr. McClain, wanting to share the light moment with him, and she felt the smile slide from her face as his stormy eyes collided with hers. The heat and volatility there frightened her. The planes of his face were hardened like they'd been chiseled from stone. She busied herself by placing her napkin in her lap the way she'd seen Hetty do.

Hetty and Gus were still going at it when a serving girl

came to take their order. When she left, an awkward silence ensued.

"Nathan, is everything arranged at the church for tomorrow? Reverend Taylor expects us at noon."

"Yeah."

"What will you wear tomorrow, dear? Do you have a special gown?"

"Well, it's not new, but I consider it special."

Mr. McClain cut in unexpectedly. "You're going to need more, from what I saw of that little travel bag."

All eyes turned toward him and Sara's mouth gaped.

"How many dresses did you bring?" he demanded.

"I–I brought three. But I'm sure I can make do with—"

"You can buy some more in the morning. You'd best take care of it here, there's not much of a choice in Cedar Springs."

Hetty jumped in to smooth things over. "Oh, that sounds divine, dear. I can take you 'round the shops in the morning. Besides, you don't want to be launderin' two or three times a week."

"Really, Mr. McClain, it. . .it's no bother. I don't mind doing—"

"It's settled then. You'll go shopping with Hetty in the morning."

Sara's face heated. This man, a virtual stranger, was going to have to pay out money to outfit her. Then a new thought seeped into her mind. Perhaps he was ashamed to be seen with her. With fresh eyes, she discreetly examined her dress. The rounded white collar was a bit ragged on the edges and, if she were honest, not quite white anymore, but rather gray and dingy. The pleats that fell below her waist were sharply pressed, but the edges had faded to a chalky blue and stood out in contrast to the navy material. Even the ribbon in her hair, she knew, was worn and frayed.

Humiliation washed over her. He was embarrassed to be seen with her.

"And if we're going to be married, you'd best call me by my given name," he grumbled.

The food arrived as a rosy pink climbed her cheeks, and she was saved further embarrassment as Gus said grace. Sara watched Hetty pick up one of the forks to the left of her plate, and Sara imitated the action.

The silence of the hungry prevailed over the table and Sara was grateful for the excuse not to have to talk to Mr.—to Nathan—anymore.

Suddenly, it registered in her mind what he'd said. *If we're going to be married. . .* He did still intend to marry her. Relief, confusion, and fear battled for the lead in her head. She was relieved to have her future settled—to have some security and peace of mind. However, she couldn't conceive why Nathan, who clearly found her loathsome, wanted to marry her. His aversion to Sara frightened her and she didn't know what to expect from him. Hetty and Gus were at ease around him. But, then, he wasn't angry with *them.*

The meal continued, fragmented by bits of conversation. Sara was replacing the napkin on the table when she realized she hadn't tasted a single bite of her food, so absorbed was she in her plight.

Hetty's coffee cup rattled as she set it back on the saucer. "Sara, why don't I come to your room at 8:00 in the morning and we'll go from there."

"That sounds fine, Hetty. Thank you."

Gus stretched back in his chair. "I don't know about you-all, but I'm as tuckered as a new foal."

They agreed to turn in for the night and went their separate ways.

In her room, Sara slipped into her nightdress, blew out the lantern, then climbed into the cozy bed. She expected to lie awake, sorting through her thoughts, but the soft bed lulled her and exhaustion came, bringing with it a veil of darkness.

&

Nathan knew he'd been testy, but he was so frustrated by the turn of events that he couldn't disguise his feelings.

He punched his down pillow and turned over to face the only window in the room. The moonlight shone through the white curtains, making them almost transparent.

Why hadn't he just settled for Laura Reed? He could have dealt with her nosy mother. Even Mara Lawton would have been easier to live with. No, he wouldn't go that far. But at least there was no chance he'd grow fond of *her,* even as pretty as she was. It was no secret she would have married him, if he'd asked her, but God help the man who would have to live with her.

Sara's image surfaced in his mind. Mara didn't hold a candle to her. Sara's midnight-blue eyes were fringed by long dark lashes and set under a pair of finely arched brows. A tiny mouth that reminded him of a child's matched her cheeks when a rosy blush swept across them.

Yes, her appearance disturbed him, but that wasn't all that bothered him. She had a helpless quality about her that made him instinctively want to protect her, and that went against all his plans for this marriage. He didn't want her depending on him, any more than he wanted to depend on her.

He must remain detached. It wouldn't be easy at the beginning, but once she got the notion, it would work out. He had no choice now. What could he say? *"My apologies, Miss Donaldson, but you're too beautiful and too desirable, so I'm afraid I can't marry you after all."*

He supposed the good Lord must know what He was doing. Nathan's favorite Scripture, Romans 8:28, came to mind and he silently considered it. *"And we know that all things work together for good to them that love God, to them who are the called according to his purpose."* Well, that was some comfort.

Still, if it hadn't been for Pop and that will, he wouldn't be in this mess in the first place.

Nathan punched his pillow again and heaved his body over to face the door. He had a feeling it was going to be a long night.

five

The next morning arrived with the promise of a fine spring day. Outside, the birds were singing their praises and the sun was playing peekaboo behind white puffy clouds against a backdrop of blue.

Sara and Hetty had shopped all morning and, despite the awkwardness of spending Nathan's money, Sara had had a splendid time. Sara's spirits were lighter today, perhaps because she had yet to see Nathan. She delighted in Hetty's companionship and knew they would get on well in the years to come.

Years. It seemed impossible to imagine this marriage lasting a lifetime. Was she fooling herself to even think it could? Even marriages based on love required hard work, she was sure. How could she expect lifetime commitment from a man she'd only met once?

Hetty seemed oblivious to Sara's deep thoughts as they shopped. In fact, Hetty seemed to enjoy the excursion immensely. She knew the latest fashions and served as an advisor as Sara tried on dresses. They'd settled on three. One was lilac, one the color of an apricot, and the fanciest one was in a shade of russet. Sara had never spent so much money at one time in all her life. Her pangs of guilt were assuaged by ever-practical Hetty, who insisted she was simply purchasing the bare necessities. Besides, she was adamant about not wanting to embarrass Nathan with her appearance; she would make him proud to call her his wife.

They concluded their morning with a cup of coffee in the hotel dining room.

"You're gonna be needin' to get ready for the weddin' soon, Sara. Would you like some help?"

"Oh, yes, Hetty, please. You're so thoughtful."

"Nonsense. It's your weddin' day. Anyhow, I'm gettin' somethin' out of this marriage, too. I've been at that ranch for the last eleven years with no female companionship. It's gonna be heavenly to have someone to chat with during the day. And a Christian, to boot! I figure I'm truly the lucky one in all this."

Sara's smile froze on her face, and she took her last sip of coffee to chase away the awkwardness. She hadn't figured on that little fib being such an issue. She believed in God, of course, and she'd attended church occasionally with her mama. It had all seemed like a history lesson to her. The preacher had dwelled on this Jesus and His gruesome death. Sara didn't see why he'd had to linger over that unfortunate event. It was all so long ago, and so irrelevant now.

She'd just attend church with the other three, bow her head for grace, and nod her head a lot when the subject of religion came up. How hard could it be? She'd learn about their religion as time passed. Until then, she would just be careful to avoid getting into the specifics of their beliefs. Luckily, her mama had raised her to be an upstanding young woman, so she wouldn't have to alter her personality or anything.

Hetty graciously paid for the coffee, then said she'd meet Sara in her room in a moment.

By the time Hetty tapped on her door, Sara had on her ivory gown. She opened the door to see Hetty clutching a bouquet of spring flowers and a small spray of crocus for Sara's hair.

Sara received the flowers and showed her in. "You've thought of everything! You've been so kind, Hetty. Thank you!"

"Not at all, dear, I was happy to do it. I do love a good weddin'! Now, turn about and let me see you." Sara did a modest pirouette. "Just as I thought. You look glorious! Let's try your hair down, though; how does that sound?"

"Oh, no, I can't!" A hand flew to her hair. She couldn't let him see her wild hair down. "I mean, I really prefer to wear it up. Look, we can put the blossoms here, in the back."

"Well, okay, if you think that's best. I just adore long, curly hair, though. I'd venture yours is lovely all down around your shoulders."

Sara surrendered the flowers to Hetty, who pinned them in her hair.

Since the church was just a short walk from the hotel, they'd agreed to meet Nathan and Gus there. Hetty insisted that Nathan shouldn't see Sara before the ceremony. It was only "right proper," she'd said.

Hetty made another adjustment to Sara's hair, then they began their walk to the church. When they reached the street, nerves began to set in. Sara's legs wobbled like a rickety chair, and her heart fluttered at twice its normal pace. In thirty minutes she'd be a married woman. Oh, she hoped he wouldn't be angry today. His stony silence had unsettled her terribly. Perhaps he'd be pleased with her since she'd done her best with her appearance. One thing was for certain: She could not look any better than she did right now. Each attribute was displayed to its best effect, from her carefully upswept hair to her stockinged feet.

Hetty tried to maintain a conversation, but Sara's heart just wasn't in it, so Hetty let her agonize in peace.

Soon they approached the small chapel. The wood

building was painted white and topped with a bell tower. Clusters of trees bearing new green foliage isolated the church from the rest of the town.

When they entered the church, Sara allowed her eyes to adjust to the dim light while Hetty laid her hat and reticule on a shelf in the cloakroom.

Their rustling must have alerted the men to their presence, for when they rounded the corner of the sanctuary, three pairs of eyes were fixed on them. Hetty fell back and let Sara precede her down the aisle.

Light filtered through the stained-glass windows, casting a golden glow on three men gathered at the altar. Nathan's face revealed admiration, and Sara's face began to relax in a nervous smile. But when she drew closer, she saw that the dimness must have deceived her, for Nathan's face was as harsh and unyielding as the day before. Gray eyes went blank as he turned away.

Her floundering spirits found reprieve in Gus's wide grin. "Sara, you're prettier than the first spring blossom, ain't she, Nathan?"

"Sure, she looks fine," he said without looking.

Somehow he made the compliment sound insulting. The pains she'd taken with her dress and coiffure were wasted on this man who clearly found her revolting. An uncharacteristic flash of defiance made her wish she'd worn her hair down, just to spite him.

When they reached the altar, Sara joined Nathan in the center facing the reverend, while Hetty and Gus took their places. Nathan gestured to a short, balding man. "Sara, this is Reverend Taylor. Reverend, meet Sara Donaldson."

Reverend Taylor smiled and pumped Sara's hand. "Soon to be Mrs. McClain, right Miss Donaldson?" His eyes twinkled.

A pink blush swept across her face. "A pleasure to meet you."

The reverend opened his Bible and patted the stuffing around his middle. "Shall we begin?" He paused as Nathan nodded once.

He read some Scripture related to marriage, then stopped to pray. Sara's thoughts were tumbling to and fro. She hadn't even been able to follow the reverend's words.

They raised their heads as the prayer ended, and Reverend Taylor instructed Sara and Nathan to face one another. When she turned, she noticed for the first time that he was attired in a suit. She fixed her eyes on the second button of the crisp white shirt.

The reverend continued. "Nathan, take Sara's left hand." Sara transferred the bouquet to her right hand and yielded her left hand to Nathan, hoping he wouldn't notice its trembling.

"You may slide the ring on her finger and repeat after me," said the reverend. Nathan received a ring from Gus and slid it on her ring finger.

Sara gaped at the ring. It was old, perhaps a family heirloom, and its fiery diamond was set between two sapphires. The delicate band widened to a fan on both sides of the blue stones. As if through a tunnel, she heard Nathan repeat his vows. His voice was deep and, although Sara avoided his gaze, his words sounded sincere.

Sara met Nathan's eyes as he completed his vows. Next it was her turn, and her voice trembled as she delivered the words that would bind her to Nathan for life. When she finished, they turned to Reverend Taylor, who said, "I now pronounce you man and wife. What God hath joined together, let no man tear asunder. Nathan, you may kiss your bride."

Sara's head swung around, and her lips parted in surprise, for in all the excitement, she'd forgotten about this part of the ceremony. Apparently Nathan had not, for he didn't seem the least bit flustered.

As she looked at Nathan, he dipped his head, and their mouths joined briefly. His lips were surprisingly warm and soft, and what she expected to be a disagreeable experience was a pleasant one indeed. When he withdrew, their eyes locked. There was a softness to his face that she hadn't seen before. She absorbed the warmth in his half-shut eyes and the room shrunk to exclude all others. The spell was broken when the reverend spoke.

"Allow me to present Mr. and Mrs. Nathan McClain," he said with a flourish.

Hetty hugged them, and there were handshakes and smiles all around as the group said good-bye to the reverend, then strolled out to the carriage.

It was one of those moments that seemed otherworldly—almost as if it weren't really happening. Perhaps this was because the experience was so out of the ordinary for her. After all, it wasn't every day she married a stranger!

When they reached the carriage, Nathan helped his wife up, and they started toward the hotel to collect their luggage.

Nathan's mind swam as he led the team onto the road. Somehow, last night as he tossed and turned, he'd convinced himself that Sara wasn't as becoming as he'd thought. But today, when she walked down the aisle toward him, he realized what a featherbrain he'd been. His wife was a rare beauty. He should have known that if she'd managed to look so appealing yesterday, after traveling for days, she would look even better after a good night's rest. A part of him was proud to have her as his wife. After all, what man wouldn't be honored to have such a beauty on his arm?

She'd looked wispy and fragile in that frothy getup. Her eyes had been wide and wary as she'd studied him, and he knew he'd let his guard down for a moment, had seen the relief in her face, before he'd replaced his impassive mask.

His resolve had paid off throughout the ceremony, but when his lips touched hers, his intentions shattered. Her timid response shook him clear down to his fancy boots. He'd never been so affected by a simple kiss—had never felt a woman quiver at his touch and felt so virile for being able to elicit such a response. Her hair smelled of lilacs and she tasted as vibrant as spring. It took tremendous effort to damper himself down once again.

If he had any hopes of continuing his plan, he must avoid kissing her again.

"Oh, look!" Sara whispered, pointing at a gaunt, emaciated dog ambling along the side of the road. Nathan pulled the carriage to a stop at the hotel's entrance. "It doesn't look like he's eaten in weeks."

Nathan strode into the hotel to collect the baggage, and Sara stepped down from her seat to approach the dog.

"Careful, Sara, don't get yourself bit," Hetty said.

Sara stooped down and extended her hand. The coal-colored animal paused to sniff it, then nuzzled his face in her hand. His dry nose was coated with dust.

Sara laughed. "Look, he likes me!"

"He surely does. Poor, wretched creature. Someone must have turned him out weeks ago, by the look of it." Hetty reached in the saddlebag and drew out two slices of bread. Gus handed them down to Sara.

"Here you go, boy," Sara said. The dog devoured the treat. "Mercy, you are a hungry one, huh, fella?" Sara caressed the dusty fur coat and murmured sweet words in the animal's ear.

Moments later, this was how Nathan found them as he exited the hotel. Nathan stopped beside the dog. "What's going on?"

Sara popped up to her feet, her eyes wide with caution. "I, um. . .I was just giving the dog a bite to eat. He was famished."

Nathan began to load the bags into the carriage, and his ambivalence bolstered Sara's courage.

"Nathan?"

"What is it?"

"Could I. . .that is, do you think it would be possible to take him back to the ranch? The dog, I mean. He's so bony, and someone clearly must have abandoned him."

Nathan turned his head away and squinted his eyes as he mulled over Sara's appeal.

His hesitation gave her renewed hope. "He won't be any problem, I promise you. I will take full responsibility for him."

Nathan turned suddenly, his face hard and forbidding, and advanced on her. She retreated, nearly tripping in the process, her heart thudding in the cavity of her chest.

But he stopped when he reached the wary animal. Crouching down, he offered his hand to the dog, then, having gained its approval, Nathan gathered the dog in his arms and set him on the floor of the carriage.

Sara watched in stunned silence. For a moment she'd thought she'd pushed him beyond his level of tolerance by asking a favor of him. But instead, he'd acceded to her request. What a confusing man he was. She wondered if she'd ever figure him out.

Hetty leaned forward to pet the attention-starved dog as Nathan turned to give Sara a hand up. Her features were earnest and bewildered as she spoke. "Thank you, Nathan."

He helped her up. "Just see to it he's taken care of," he muttered, and pulled the brim of his hat down low as he walked around the carriage.

six

They headed eastward, leaving Wichita and setting off for Cedar Springs. Once they left the city, they passed farms and ranches, which gradually were spaced farther apart. A good ways out of town there was only an occasional sod hut to betray the presence of human life.

Green hills rose majestically in the distance, and trees were scattered about as though someone had dropped the seeds at random. Recent rain had made the grasslands spring-green, and periodically they saw cattle dotting the landscape.

Sara knew she would have no trouble adapting to life in Kansas. At the moment, Boston seemed like another lifetime, and she was happy to have it remain so.

During the long ride, Hetty told Sara about Cedar Springs and the ranch. Their town sounded quaint. It boasted a mill, church, post office, grocery, feed and seed, and carriage works. Roughly two hundred people had settled the area surrounding the town—mostly farmers and ranchers. Cedar Springs was a mere ten-minute ride from the ranch.

Hetty told her about various people, too, most of whom attended church with them. The names all blended together in Sara's mind, but she was sure she would soon put faces and names together.

The dog was curled up at Sara's feet, undisturbed by the jostling wagon. Sara reached down to stroke the dull black fur.

"What are you gonna call him, Sara?" Hetty asked from the backseat.

"I don't know just yet. Do you have any ideas?"

Gus laughed. "Oughta name him 'Bones.' I can count his ribs just by lookin' at him."

Hetty gave him a sideways glance. "You're a fine one to talk, Gus Fenton! Besides, by the time me and Sara fatten him up, 'Pudgy' might be more fittin'!"

The three of them laughed and carried on, making up names, each more silly than the one before it. By the time they were done, Sara decided on plain "Blackie." Once she washed the filth from his coat, it would be ink black, she knew.

His nose was resting on the top of her boot, and his eyes were closed in the sleep of the secure. She'd never had a pet before and relished the idea of having something to take care of—something to depend on her, to love her. He would keep her company and fill the void that her marriage left.

She'd hoped for a normal marriage. Not a love match, of course, but a partnership based on friendship and respect. It wasn't to be, however. Judging by Nathan's reaction to her, this was to be a marriage in name only. A man didn't want to fulfill his fleshly desires with a woman he found repulsive. Her face heated with embarrassment at the wicked thought. She could be thankful for that, she supposed.

Hetty's next words were so similar to her thoughts that she wondered if her rosy cheeks had given them away.

"I fixed up Nathan's old room for you, Sara. He moved into his Daddy's room several days ago to make room for you. There's another room as well, but it was meant to be a nursery, and it's small as a squirrel's nest."

"You didn't have to go to all that trouble. I'm accustomed to a small room."

"Wasn't no trouble at all. Anyway, it would be a waste

to have that big room sit empty." Hetty pointed to a barbed-wire fence. "See that fence? That's the western border of the ranch. Just a little ways to go."

They drove on, around a bend and down a hill. Nathan turned right onto a rutted drive. The wooden sign above the drive read "McClain Ranch" in white letters. About a hundred yards to the left of the drive a creek swept by. In the same direction, beyond the creek, was a high ridge of hills, covered in bluestem grass and stippled with grazing cattle. There were trees scattered throughout, and along the creek bank, willows and cottonwood were thriving. Off to the right was a band of prairie grass, spreading across two hundred yards or so, then another chain of hills.

Sara could see the house and barns off in the distance. They lay nestled, like a sleeping baby, between the two hilly ridges.

"Sure is good to be home," Hetty said. "That hotel was right fancy, but there's nothin' like your own bed and your own kitchen!"

Moments later they climbed wearily from the carriage and stretched their stiff limbs. Sara's backside ached from being jostled on the wood seat. Blackie bounced down with renewed energy and raised his nose skyward, smelling the air with acute interest. They left him to his exploring and went into the white two-story house.

It was much larger and tidier than Sara's house in Boston. Handwoven rugs were carefully arranged on the polished wood floor. The main room was to the left and was sprinkled with a hodgepodge of comfortable-looking furniture. A stone fireplace dominated the far wall. Straight ahead, a hand-carved banister flanked the stairs leading to the second story. The dining room, to the right, featured a wooden table and chairs. Beyond the dining area was a door that she presumed led to the kitchen. Directly to the right of the staircase, along the far wall, was another door, which Sara hoped was a water closet!

The heat of the sun filtered in through white eyelet curtains, making the house warm and bright.

"You have a lovely home, Nathan. Have you always lived here?"

"Yeah. My dad and granddad built it. Excuse me, I need to go change and check on the livestock." Nathan disappeared up the stairs.

"I'll meet you at the barn," Gus called.

After they left, Hetty turned to Sara. "So tell me, dear . . .how do you like the McClain ranch? Do you find it agreeable?"

"It's more than agreeable! The house is so spacious and cozy. And the land! Hilly and green. . .wide-open space." Her face was animated with undisguised excitement.

Hetty cocked an eyebrow. "So, you don't think you'll mind livin' so far away from the city?"

"I've been longing to get away from the city for as long as I've lived there. This is like heaven to me."

"Well, I wouldn't go that far! After all, the Bible says in 1 Corinthians 2:9, 'Eye hath not seen, nor ear heard, neither have entered into the heart of man, the things which God hath prepared for them that love him.' "

"Um, that's right. Would you mind terribly if I rested for a while? I'm afraid I didn't sleep well on the train, and I'm exhausted."

"You don't have to ask. This is your house now! Let me show you where your room is."

At the top of the stairs they turned right.

"Nathan's room is on the other side of the stairs." Hetty opened Sara's door. "Here we are."

Gauzy yellow curtains draped the window on the far wall. A bureau stood against the left wall, and across from it was a small, high bed covered with a colorful quilt. A large oval rug stretched over the plank floor. It was clean and welcoming, and Sara immediately felt at home.

Sara set her bag by the bureau. "Hetty, would you mind putting out some food and water for Blackie?"

"I'll do it right now. You have a good rest. Supper's at 6:00. Oh! I hope you don't mind, Sara, but I mentioned the idea of a little bridal shower to a few of the ladies at church. I was thinkin' of havin' it here, maybe next Saturday?"

"Oh. That's very thoughtful, Hetty. Thank you. I'm sure next Saturday would be just fine."

After Hetty left, Sara slipped out of her ivory gown and hung it carefully on a peg. Pulling back the quilt, she climbed into the bed and curled up under the covers. The bed and room were new to her, but she was sure this would feel like home soon enough.

Sara nervously chewed at her lip as she lay waiting for her mind to settle. It was generous of Hetty to plan a shower for her, but she really wished she didn't have to go through with it. She had never been one to like being the center of attention. Particularly when all the guests were strangers to her. Well, there was nothing to be done about it now.

Sara woke in time to help Hetty with supper. Nathan and Gus had spent the afternoon working outside. Their neighbors, Luke and Caleb, had watched over the ranch in their absence.

At 6:00, the men came in just as the food was being placed on the table, and they took their seats. Nathan was at the head of the table, Hetty and Gus to his left, and Sara to his right. The food was tasty and the company delightful—

except for Nathan, who kept mostly to himself.

Sara dreaded the time when Gus and Hetty would retire to their home, leaving her alone with Nathan. He'd been avoiding her since their initial meeting, and she didn't want to irritate him with her presence. She felt it would be rude, however, to excuse herself and hide away in her room, especially since she'd spent the afternoon there. Perhaps Hetty and Gus would keep them company for a while.

When they'd taken their last bites and conversation had petered out, she and Hetty cleared the table and washed the dishes. Hetty hung the towel to dry when they finished. "You ready, Gus?" she called.

"Anytime you are, darlin'."

"We'll see ya in the mornin', Sara. We leave for church at half past eight, but I'll be over to start breakfast at seven."

"All right, Hetty. I'll see you then."

"Night." Nathan sank into the fireside chair and opened a newspaper.

As they left, Sara caught sight of Blackie on the porch, and an idea took form in her mind.

"Nathan," she said timidly.

"Hmm?"

"I, um. . .if I give Blackie a bath, would it be all right to bring him into the house? At night, I mean?"

"It's your house, too. Do what you like."

Relieved to have something to do, Sara went to collect the tin tub she'd seen under the kitchen shelves. She hauled the container and soap to the yard and pumped water into it. Dusk was descending upon the valley, and streaks of pink smeared the horizon.

Blackie scampered around her, oblivious to the inevitable moment when he would be submerged in the cool water.

"Come here, Blackie." She awkwardly scooped him into her arms and deposited him in the tub. His paws had no sooner touched the water than he was jumping to get out.

"Whoa, boy!" Sara grabbed the sopping wet dog just as he started to leap, and held him. "Now, I know this isn't going to be any fun for you, but you're a filthy dirty doggie, and if you want to come in the house tonight, you must cooperate. That's it." She continued to hold him while she ran the soap across his back. "There now. That's not so bad, is it?"

She leaned back to put the soap down, and Blackie came leaping out of the tub in a spray of cold water. He shook himself, his sodden fur flinging drops of water all over her already-wet dress. "Oh! You naughty dog!"

She dove for him, and missed, as he scooted away. Finally she captured him and dumped him in the water. For the remainder of the bath she maintained a tight hold on the dog. The sun was down and darkness had descended by the time they went into the house, both of them wet and tired.

❧

Nathan turned the page of the *Wichita Eagle,* then sat back and scanned it with weary eyes. It had been quite a day. He was glad Hetty and Sara were getting on so well. They would be good company for each other. Thank goodness for Hetty and Gus. He couldn't imagine trying to pull this off without them. Just having their conversation at suppertime was a distraction worth the cost of their salaries.

After supper was another matter altogether. It would be odd having someone around in the evening when he was used to quiet and solitude. Of course, she wasn't really around tonight; she was outside. Clearly she preferred the dog's company to his—not that he could blame her, given the way he'd been behaving. This was the way it was supposed to work anyhow. She'd keep to herself, and he'd keep to himself.

He realized he'd been staring blankly at the paper, so he tossed it on the floor. He ambled over to the window and peered through the curtains to see how Sara was doing with the dog.

The corner of Nathan's mouth lifted as he saw her struggling to put the dog into the tub. That furball might be skin and bones, but he was twice Sara's size. He tried to leap out when she plopped him into the water. Nathan's lips formed a full grin when she seized the dog in a hug. She appeared to be reasoning with him and must have thought she convinced him to stay in the tub, for she leaned away from him.

The dog came bounding out of the water with a splash, giving Sara a bath in the process. Nathan chuckled. Apparently she'd never given a dog a bath before. At least not one as reluctant to be bathed as that one. When she dove for the sopping mutt and landed flat in the dirt, Nathan roared with laughter.

He knew he should help her, and he'd just started to move away from the window when she captured the dog and deposited him back in the water. Nathan had a feeling she wouldn't be letting go of him anytime soon.

Shaking his head, he made his way to his room. She sure had some spunk for such a tiny thing.

seven

Sara woke to the slam of the door. It was Pete, she knew. *Please don't let him come in here.* She wished once again for a lock on her door and momentarily thought of shoving the chest against the door. Remembering the one time she'd tried it before kept her on the bed.

She curled up, tucking the covers beneath her chin, and waited. Soon she heard the thumping of his feet as he ascended to the second floor. There were eight steps, and she counted his footfalls, mentally measuring his progress. He stumbled on the seventh step and banged heavily against the wall. A crashing noise followed, and Sara knew it was her mother's portrait falling down the stairs.

There was a moment of silence as Pete recovered his balance at the top of the stairs.

Turn right. . .just this once!

Sara breathed in quiet, shallow breaths and kept perfectly still. *Maybe if he thinks I'm asleep. . .*

But it was not to be. She heard him coming toward her door and squeezed her eyes shut. The door crashed open and ricocheted off the wall. Instinct spurred Sara into action and she scrambled across the bed to the far corner of the room. Moonlight glowed through the tattered cotton drapes, casting sinister shadows on Pete's horrid face.

She crouched in the corner and buried her head against the peeling wallpaper.

Pete's stumbling footsteps echoed through the room. Sara heard whimpering and knew it was her own.

His brutal hands grabbed her hair and yanked her upward. "Please. . .no. . .no!"

Sara jerked awake. Her heart throbbed madly and she looked around the blackened room. Where was she? Where was Pete? Slowly the vague shapes of furniture came into focus.

She was at the ranch. Sara sagged with relief. Hetty, Gus, Nathan. The ranch. Her eyes searched the floor and she spotted Blackie's sleeping form huddled on the carpet beside her bed. At least she hadn't awakened anyone with screaming.

Wiping her damp forehead, Sara turned on her side and tried to slow her breathing. She was safe enough. There was a lock on her door here, and she knew enough to use it! Pete was far away and couldn't hurt her now. She repeated the thought over and over until she drifted off to sleep.

❧

Sara rose at dawn the following morning, feeling the groggy remnants of last night's dream. Staying in bed was tempting, but she wanted to ready herself for church, then get breakfast started before Hetty came.

She donned her new russet gown, which Hetty had persuaded her to buy. Sara thought she looked like a weed regardless of what she wore, but Hetty said the dress showed off her slim figure.

In the kitchen, she put on an apron, started the coffee, and began to make biscuits, using her mother's recipe. Finding her way around the kitchen was easy enough since everything was exactly where she would have put it. By the time Hetty arrived, Sara was ready to bake the biscuits.

"Well, now, look who's up bright and early! And got a start on breakfast, too! I'm not used to all this spoilin'!"

"Good morning, Hetty. I've been idle for days, what

with all the traveling. It feels good to be doing something productive."

Hetty started the bacon and eggs and told Sara about their church. Gus arrived next, in his Sunday best.

"Mornin', Sara."

"Good morning." Sara watched as Blackie trotted over to greet Gus.

"Looks as if someone had a bath! You cleaned up real nice, little feller. Still scrawny, but I think there's hope for ya! You give 'im a bath, Sara?"

"Must we talk about it? I never dreamed it would be such a trial! I'm not certain who looked sillier—Blackie or me!"

"I'd cast my vote on you." Nathan stood leaning arrogantly against the doorway to the dining room.

Sara's eyes darted to his as her mouth fell open. His face was serious, but something in his eyes hinted of mockery. Her mouth shut with a snap as color suffused her face. She made herself busy with the food. He must have watched from the window. She reviewed the episode in her mind and saw what he must have seen—her struggle, her drenching, her sprawling! Oh, the mortification!

Gus watched the heat spread across her cheeks. "That musta been some bath!"

"You two leave this poor girl alone! Breakfast is ready; now, take your seats." Hetty served up the bacon and eggs while Sara put the biscuits on the table.

They seated themselves at the table, said grace, and turned their thoughts to food, much to Sara's relief. Mostly, they talked about church and religious matters, so she remained silent and pretended to be interested in her food.

After Sara and Hetty washed dishes, they all boarded the carriage and set off for church. The short ride passed quickly, and soon Sara glimpsed the small white church. The sign above the door read, "Cedar Springs Church of God."

As they entered the building, she noted that there were twenty or so people seated on the wooden benches. There were rows on both sides of them as they proceeded up the aisle and took their seats near the front. The interior was rather plain, compared to the other two churches she'd been in, with colorless windows on the east and west sides of the building. The pews were polished to a shine, but lacked the ornamental carving of the church where her mother had attended.

Nathan said hello to a few friends as he passed, but the quiet chattering completely ceased as they took their seats. Sara's face grew warm as she felt the curious gazes pierce her back. Hetty had said she'd mentioned her to a few of the women, but it was obvious from the looks she was receiving that some were wondering who she was. Did they suspect she was Nathan's new wife? Surely they didn't know about the ad in the paper? *Oh! Why didn't I think to ask Hetty?* She fought against the urge to squirm in her seat.

She kept her eyes focused on the pulpit until the song leader stepped forward. Hetty whispered that this was their neighbor, Luke. He was tall and thin, with wavy hair that matched his buckeye-brown eyes.

There were no songbooks, but Sara knew some of the words, so she attempted to sing along. The reverend stepped forward after the song. He had a medium build and thick, ashen hair that was cut above the collar.

Other than the man who had married them, Sara had only known one other preacher, and his sermons had been as tiresome and severe as he was. But Reverend Hill was as dissimilar from that as he could be. He told captivating stories, and he had a way of making one see things from a whole new angle.

He talked of God's creation and how diverse and magnificent it was: a myriad of textures and smells, a rainbow of colors, sounds that ranged from high to low, and food that ran the gamut from salty to sweet. He spoke of how God could have made His creation bland and boring, but loved everyone so much that He gave His children the best—a creation people could enjoy and savor. Sara had never considered this before. She'd always imagined that God was detached and impersonal.

When the reverend stopped to say the closing prayer, Sara realized her mind hadn't strayed once, as it always had in Boston. She was pleased that Reverend Hill was such a gifted speaker, especially since she would be required to sit through a sermon every week!

"Amen." Nathan echoed the preacher's closing word and the crowd rose to leave.

"How'd ya like the message, Sara?" Hetty asked.

"It was very interesting. Your pastor is a skillful speaker."

"Don't I know it! Why, I could just listen to him all day. Hello, Laura! I'd like you to meet Sara."

A young woman had walked over to their pew. She held a hand out to Sara. "I'm pleased to meet you, Sara. It will be lovely to have someone else my age here in Cedar Springs to visit with."

"Thank you. You're very kind."

"Laura's a good friend of mine," Nathan said. "We went to school together most of our lives."

"I've got a story or two I could tell you, Sara!"

Nathan stretched up to his full height. "Laura Reed, don't you go filling her head with a bunch of nonsense. . ."

"Excuse me!" A short, round woman bustled over to them. "Oh! You must be Nathan's new wife; why, I've just been dyin' to meet ya! Saw ya walk in, and I thought 'that must be her.' Everyone is just so curious about—"

"Ma, please! You're embarrassing her." Laura looked at Sara. "This is my mother, Mrs. Reed."

Sara shook her hand. "How do you do?"

"Come on, Ma. We need to go ask Reverend and Mrs. Hill over for dinner."

"But, I really wanted to—"

"Come on, Ma!" Laura nearly had to drag Mrs. Reed away. Sara was flustered by all the attention and hoped that Mrs. Reed would not be attending the shower!

Gus shook his head. "I don't know how that woman managed to raise such a sweet child."

"She means well. She's just. . .curious," Hetty said.

Gus snorted. "I think meddlin' is the word you're lookin' for!"

"Now, that's enough!" Hetty said. "Let's make our way out, so Sara can meet Reverend Hill."

Several people stopped them on their way out, including Mrs. Hill. She was a plump woman with silver-gray hair and rosy cheeks that accentuated her friendly smile.

The reverend stood at the door shaking hands with his congregation. "Hello, Hetty, Gus. Nice to see you. Nathan, introduce me to your lovely wife."

"This is Sara, Reverend. Sara, meet Reverend Hill."

"It's a pleasure meeting you," Sara said.

"The pleasure's all mine, Sara. I hope I can look forward to your presence every Sunday."

"Of course."

"Wonderful! Well, I must go collect the missus. We've been invited to the Reeds' for dinner."

Gus chortled. "My sincere regrets!"

Hetty poked him in the ribs, and the reverend gave a delightful chuckle as he walked away.

Moments later, in the swaying wagon, Sara found herself unable to contain her contented smile. She loved the ranch with its rolling green hills and towering trees. The town of Cedar Springs was small and quaint, offering all the necessities with none of the commotion. Even most of the people she'd met were warm and engaging.

If only the strain between her and her husband would disappear. . .

eight

The next week Sara began to establish a new routine. She and Hetty prepared breakfast at dawn. After that, Nathan and Gus went out to work and usually didn't return until suppertime. The women packed the men a lunch to eat out in the pasture so they wouldn't have to ride back in for lunch.

During the day, she and Hetty cleaned, did the washing, made bread, mended, and did whatever else needed to be done. Much of it they did together, but Hetty went to her own home for some of the chores. This was just as well, since Sara had always enjoyed having time to herself.

By the end of the week it became clear to Sara that Hetty had been doing all the chores before her arrival— even all the meals. Therefore, Sara began to wonder why Nathan had sought out a wife. When she'd responded to his ad, she'd assumed he wanted a wife for the ordinary reasons—companionship and a helpmate. Certainly someone to cook and clean and to look after the home. She had come here expecting to carry out those duties.

Of course, it had become plain to her after meeting him that it wasn't companionship he sought! At least not from her. She knew she'd failed in that way; she clearly was not what he'd wanted in a woman. She had come to terms with this in Wichita, and had anticipated the chance to make amends by being a proper helpmate. On the long drive to Cedar Springs, she'd pictured a house that needed loving care, holey socks that needed mending, and floors

57

that needed scrubbing. These things she could do, and do well.

But those things had not even been neglected. Hetty had been taking care of Nathan's home. And so, it was with all this on her mind that she decided to approach Hetty.

The day was pleasantly warm, with just enough breeze to keep the temperature perfect. They were finishing the washing in the front yard. Hetty ran the clothes through the wringer, while Sara hung them on the line to dry. They had been working in mutual silence.

"Hetty?" Sara asked.

"Umm?"

"Do you. . .that is. . .why did Nathan marry me?"

Hetty stopped wringing midturn and looked at her with raised brows. "What?"

"I mean. . .well, Nathan must have told you how we came to meet, right?"

"You mean the advertisement? Yes, he told us."

"Well. . .a man doesn't just place an ad like that without some thought. He must want a marriage—a wife—for some reason. . .don't you think?"

"Of course he wanted a wife! He'd hardly have gone to all that trouble if he didn't."

"That. . .that's what I thought from the outset, but. . ."

"What's troublin' ya, dear?"

"It's just that. . . See, you've always done the cooking and cleaning for Nathan, haven't you? Taken care of his home and everything?"

"Well, yes, that's always been part of my job."

"And you've seen the way Nathan. . .the way he doesn't . . . Well, he plainly doesn't even like me!"

"Sara! That's just not true! Now, I know he's been a little gruff. Okay, a lot gruff. But it's not you, dear. You see,

Nathan's daddy died some months back, and he's just not been the same since. Still grievin', I guess. He's never had a mama—she died birthin' him. So, ya see. . .he's got no family left. I expect he wanted a wife so he wouldn't be all alone in the world. Oh, sure, he's got me an' Gus, but we've got our own family scattered across the country. Besides, it's natural for a man his age to start wantin' some young'uns."

Sara flushed a deep red and hung a shirt on the line. She wasn't even going to pursue that topic!

"I think, if ya just give 'im a little time, he'll come around. He didn't used to walk around in a snit all the time!"

They laughed and resumed the laundry. Sara felt she had a better understanding of Nathan now. He must miss his father the way she missed her mama. Maybe Hetty was right; she'd just give it some time.

❧

On Saturday Sara woke with a sigh of resignation. Shower day. All the women were coming around noon for a potluck luncheon. Even though they were planning to eat outdoors, she and Hetty had scoured the floors and put an extra polish on everything that shines in preparation for the guests.

Sara had tried to act excited about the event. She didn't want to hurt Hetty's feelings, after all, but she was really uneasy about being thrust upon this group of women whom she didn't even know. Well, that wasn't entirely true. Mrs. Hill, the reverend's wife, would be coming, along with Laura and her mother. She would just smile graciously and try to make small talk with the others—not one of her better abilities.

After Nathan and Gus finished their morning chores,

they set up three tables outside in the shade of a large oak tree. Hetty fluttered about, covering the tables with her own tablecloths, while Sara wandered off to gather fresh flowers for the centerpieces.

When she returned it was nearly noon, and the men had made themselves scarce.

Hetty stood back and surveyed their work. "I must say, it looks like a right cozy setup. And the Lord surely did provide us with a beautiful day! Sunny and warm with just a little breeze to cool the skin."

Sara was spared from having to answer by the clickety-clack of an approaching wagon. The first genuine smile of the day formed on her lips. It was Laura and her mother. At least she would know her first guests and be spared the awkwardness that hovered around when she was with strangers. How she longed for Helen's buffering presence!

"Happy bridal shower!" Laura exclaimed as she alighted from the wagon with a small brown package.

Hetty and Sara approached them and Laura gathered Sara in an embrace. "What a perfect day for a party!" She extended the gift toward Sara. "Every new bride needs to have her own things! At least that's what Mama's always telling me."

Mrs. Reed rounded the wagon. "Truer words were never spoken! Why, I've been sewing for years just to make certain my Laura has a fine supply of linens and such, but at this rate, our home will be overrun with them before she ever marries!"

Sara cringed inwardly as she watched heat spread over her new friend's face.

Hetty broke the tension. "Good day, Mrs. Reed, Laura! Can I get you a nice glass of tea while we wait for the others?"

Hetty took Mrs. Reed to the food table and left Laura

with Sara to chat a while. Before long there was a good-sized group of women mingling and laughing around the tables. Sara scanned the gathering for Hetty, thinking it was about time to start serving the food, but her eyes stopped on an approaching carriage. It was a phaeton, she knew—the kind her mother's doctor in Boston had owned. Its folding top was up, shading the sole occupant from the afternoon sun. Sara wondered who in Cedar Springs owned such a fancy carriage.

Sara gave a tiny gasp when the woman alighted. She was a beautiful creature. The sides of her golden hair were swept up on top of her head and held by an elaborate hair ornament. The remainder of her glorious mane flowed down her back in a silken cascade.

As she turned to walk toward the group, her full skirt swished, drawing Sara's attention to the woman's body. She was taller than Sara and curvy in all the right places. The heaviness of her skirt made Sara wonder how she could stand it in the heat, but perhaps all the skin exposed at the neckline helped to compensate.

Sara watched as she approached Hetty, a covered dish in one arm and a gaily wrapped package in the other. Sara couldn't stop the jolt of envy she felt. The woman was perfect in appearance—everything Sara wished she herself could be. Her skin was a delicate creamy color, unmarred by even a single freckle. Her long, graceful arms extended into a pair of white lace gloves.

After Hetty relieved the young lady of her burdens, she escorted her to where Sara was standing. "Sara, I don't believe you've met Mara Lawton. Her family owns the carriage works shop in town."

Sara's smile faded slightly when she met Mara's cold blue gaze. "Nice to meet you, Mara. It was so kind of you to come," she repeated for the twelfth time.

Hetty called the women to order just then and offered to say grace for the meal. Sara was kept company by Laura and a Mrs. Leighton during the meal. She blushed profusely when she found out Mrs. Leighton was the postmistress, and fervently hoped that the woman was not aware of the circumstances that prompted her letters from Boston.

During lulls in conversation, Sara found her gaze wandering to Mara. There was something in her eyes whenever she looked at Sara that made her squirm with discomfort. Why she felt this way Sara didn't know, but she was certain Mara disliked her.

The meal was a pleasant blend of country dishes. It seemed everyone around these parts was an accomplished cook. Sara wasn't accustomed to eating in a formal group setting, so she imitated the way the others handled their silver and napkins. She certainly didn't want to embarrass herself or Nathan.

The afternoon heat drove the women inside, where Sara was to open her gifts. It felt odd to receive presents from people she scarcely knew, but as she opened the packages, the women seemed as delighted to be giving them as Sara was to receive them. Most of the gifts were of a decorative nature: napkin rings, a tablecloth, a sugar bowl. When Sara lifted Mara's gift, a beautifully wrapped package tied with a satin ribbon, she knew by the shape and size that it was a book. She carefully stripped away the paper, thinking it was a shame to waste it, and held the copy up to read the title.

Everyday Etiquette: How to Conduct Yourself Like a Proper Lady. Blood rushed to Sara's face.

"What is it?" A voice called. "A recipe book?"

"Oh, indeed! Every new bride should have one!"

"That's what one's female relatives are for, Mary dear."

"Which one is it, Sara?"

Sara lifted the corners of her mouth in what she hoped resembled a smile. "It. . .it's an etiquette book."

"Oh! What a unique idea, Mara."

"Yes, a useful tool, to be sure."

Sara's heart raced. "Thank you, Mara," she squeezed out and met the woman's gaze. Mara's expression was neutrally polite, but those piercing eyes were laughing at her. One eyebrow suddenly hiked up and Sara quickly reached for the next package. Why did this woman dislike her so?

The remainder of the shower passed without incident, but Sara made a point of avoiding Mara. It wasn't difficult to do since there were so many other women present. When the last of their guests left, Sara heaved a quiet sigh of relief.

❧

Three weeks had passed since the shower. Sara and Hetty were doing the mending, and Blackie was curled up at Sara's feet. He'd become a splendid companion and served as a buffer between her and Nathan in the evenings.

"Hetty, I've been wondering. . ."

Hetty looked up from the sock she was darning.

"I've noticed there's no saloon in Cedar Springs, and I didn't see one in Wichita either. Don't people in Kansas drink spirits?"

"Well, many would like to—and some do. But there's been a law against drinkin' in Kansas since 1880. It's called prohibition. There's many that's against it, but I'm thinkin' it's a fine thing. I've seen a man or two drunk, and it's no pretty sight, that's for sure."

"No, it's not. I wish it were illegal in every state. There were a lot of saloons in Boston and a lot of drinkers, too.

It's a terrible thing—what liquor does to a man."

"Yes. I think the good Lord expects a man to keep his wits about 'im." Hetty finished the sock and picked up a shirt to sew. "Speakin' of men, are you and Nathan gettin' on any better?"

Sara sighed. "It's not that we don't get along. I mean. . . well, you've seen the way he is with me. He doesn't talk to me."

"Not when me and Gus is here. But I figure that's because we're doin' all the talkin'."

"Well, when you're not here, it's as quiet as a church. I just go about my business and he goes about his. He seems angry with me all the time."

"That boy does have a temper. But I can't see why he'd be mad at you. He's prob'ly just stewin' about somethin'."

"Maybe."

Hetty glanced up at the mantle clock. "We'd best get supper on. It's nearin' 5:00."

When the men came home, they were quiet and moody. Sara didn't find out why until they were well into the meal.

"Well, are you fellas gonna tell us what's eatin' at ya? It's clear ya got somethin' on your minds."

Gus had a mouthful of food, so Nathan answered. "It's old Mr. Murphy again. His steers keep breaking our fences."

Gus stepped in. "Then we have to round 'em up and take 'em back to his property. He doesn't even fix the fence. Wasted half the day."

Hetty shook her head. "Someone oughta have a talk with that man." She looked at Sara. "Mr. Murphy's our neighbor to the south. He's gettin' up in years, but he's got a couple of ranch hands who should be takin' care of things."

Nathan drained his cup. "Could someone pass the pitcher?"

It was just to Sara's right, so she picked it up. Her hand

shook, partly from the weight of the full pitcher and partly from nerves. Milk sloshed over the rim and left a puddle on the wood, near Nathan's plate.

"Sorry. . ." She got up to get a cloth.

"Sit down—it isn't hurting anything," he said.

Sara dropped back down in her chair, her face coloring. She didn't feel much like eating after that. Mostly she stirred her food around on her plate and took an occasional bite.

Finally the meal was over. Hetty stood and carried her dishes to the kitchen. Sara noticed she was walking with a slight limp.

"Hetty, did you hurt your leg?" Sara asked as she entered the kitchen.

"No, I got a knee that acts up now and then, that's all. I was on my feet most of the day. Shoulda known better."

"Well, why don't you just go on home, then? I'll finish up here."

"These dishes won't take but a minute."

"Precisely. They won't take me any time at all, so you just scoot on home and rest that knee."

"Land sakes! You're gettin' to be as bossy as me!" Hetty said. "Thanks, though, I think I will call it a day. Gus! You 'bout ready?"

"Yep. Your knee troublin' ya?" he asked as she hobbled over.

"Yeah. Sara's finishin' up in the kitchen, so we can get on home."

They all said their good-byes, and Sara continued clearing the table as Hetty and Gus left.

She removed the empty pitcher from the table and turned to take it into the kitchen. She jumped when she saw Nathan standing right in front of her, and the pitcher fell to the floor, shattering into pieces around her feet.

"Oh, no!" She stooped down to clean the mess and as she picked up a shard of glass, it sliced across her palm, leaving a red slash. She sucked in her breath.

Nathan reached down and pulled her up by the elbows. "Here, leave the mess. You need to take care of your hand." He led her over to the basin.

"Your pitcher. . .it's ruined. . .I'm sorry! I'm so clumsy!"

He stood behind her at the basin, cupping her wrist with one hand, pumping water with the other.

"I'm sure we got another pitcher. Open your hand."

His hand felt rough against hers as cold water gushed over them. She felt his hot breath on her neck and realized how close he was standing. She'd never been so near him—had never been so near any man—and her reaction startled her. Her heart was thumping as if it would explode, and there was a strange warmth kindling in her abdomen. How could she react this way, especially when he frightened her so?

"Won't need sutures. Gonna have to keep it clean till it closes, though." He reached over and grabbed a white cloth. After drying her hand, he wrapped the thin towel around her wound. "There's some bandages in that cabinet."

"I–I'll take care of it. Thank you. . .for helping, I mean. I'm really sorry about your pitcher. . ." Her face reddened. She couldn't put two thoughts together when this man was present! Why did she have to be so awkward?

"I'll clean up the glass. You'd better get that bandaged."

Sara bustled over to get the medicine box down. By the time she had finished awkwardly wrapping her injury, with one hand, Nathan was finished. Once again he had turned in without a word—and at 7:00 in the evening.

❧

Nathan paced across the large area rug in his room. Mercy,

what that woman did to him! He couldn't even handle a little medical treatment without going all soft in the knees.

She seemed so fragile and helpless. He had instinctively helped care for her hand, but being so close to her had been a mistake. She'd been so warm, her hands so soft. And what was that scent she wore, anyway? Lilac?

He knew he should have helped her bandage her hand. She'd been struggling to do it one-handed while he was sweeping up the glass. But a man could only take so much.

He sat on his bed and tugged off his boots. This was laughable. Here he was, trapped in his room by a ninety-eight pound woman at 7:00 in the evening.

He'd been turning in early to avoid being alone with her. He hardly paid her any heed at all, and when he did make his presence known, she jumped out of her skin—like she did with the pitcher. What a nervous Nelly she was. Most likely she was wary of him because he was so terse with her. Well, it was better this way. No entanglements to worry about, no problems to fret over, no loss to grieve.

This would have to work out. He didn't have much choice now; they were married. At least the ranch was his. Mr. VanCleeves had sent him the deed after he'd received news of Nathan's marriage. Things would settle down. She'd get used to him and relax after a while. It had only been four weeks.

He picked a book up from the bedside table. He might as well pass the time with some good reading.

nine

Sunday morning services were beginning to be the high point of Sara's week. Not just the sermons, although she did enjoy those. It was a combination of things: a change of scenery, fresh air during the ride to town, and friendly people to talk with.

On this fourth trip to church, she wasn't disappointed. Reverend Hill preached a sermon that raised many questions in her mind. He talked about sin.

"We are all imperfect creatures," he said, "born of sinful men and women. Not one of us is perfect. Only Jesus lived a perfect life on this earth."

Sara thought he would go into a history lesson about the man named Jesus, like she'd heard in Boston, but he didn't.

"Even those of us who appear to be good—who are thoughtful and kind—commit sin. Many sins are hidden away where others can't see them: bitterness, envy, selfishness. Be assured, my friend, God sees it. It's sin, black and destructive. God is our only hope for salvation. We must choose Him."

Sara considered his words carefully that week. She felt as if she now held pieces to a puzzle—only, she was missing a few pieces and couldn't make out the picture.

On Tuesday of that week, she and Hetty were clearing up the breakfast dishes when Sara broached the subject.

"Hetty, what did you think of Reverend Hill's sermon Sunday?"

Hetty looked up from the pan she was scrubbing and

squinted her eyes in thought. "Let's see. . . Oh, yes—the sinner. As always, I thought he brought a fine message. Why do you ask?"

"I. . .I guess I didn't follow along very well. I mean. . .I know everyone sins. . .no one's perfect. But that's the way we're made. We couldn't be perfect even if we tried, right?"

"Umm. That's true, yes. Just as it says in Romans 3:23, 'For all have sinned, and come short of the glory of God.' But that's the reason for Christ's death on the cross. We can't be perfect, but He was."

Sara nodded as though she understood. Hetty thought she was a Christian, and she didn't want to expose herself. The questions would have to wait. Perhaps Reverend Hill would answer them in his sermons.

Hetty removed the sack of flour from the pantry shelf. "I'm glad to have someone to talk to about such things. It makes me think. Fiddlesticks! I was wantin' to make some of those yeast rolls for supper tonight, but we're short on flour."

"Do you have any at your house?"

"Nope. No need to, since I do all my bakin' here," Hetty said.

"Well, I'd be happy to walk into town and get some. It's a lovely morning, and the fresh air would do me good."

"You're a dear! I'd go myself, but I got a pile of laundry needin' done."

"I'll just go get my hat," Sara said.

"Nathan keeps some money in that jar on the mantle. It's just for this sort of thing."

After getting a few coins, Sara left the house and paused by the corrals. She'd love to ride into town on one of Nathan's fine horses, but he hadn't offered, and she didn't feel right taking one without his permission. She'd been riding since she was old enough to walk. Her father had trained horses for a wealthy man outside of Boston, and she'd had permission to ride whenever she pleased. And ride she had. After her father died, she and her mama only had two bays, and those horses were soon sold.

Now there was a whole stable full of horses, and she need only ask permission to ride them. If she could only gather the courage to do so!

She set off toward town at a brisk pace, her calico gown swishing with each step. There was a gait to her walk that hinted of her fine mood. The sky was untainted blue, and the sun gave off enough warmth that she had no need of a shawl. Only the twittering of birds disturbed the silence.

She felt free for the first time in years. Free to walk to town anytime she chose, free to make friends, free to be happy. She giggled and added a sashay to her step. It was a good thing there was no one around! They would think she had gone mad!

She began to hum tunes, and all too soon town came into view. The saws were buzzing in their efforts to slice through wood. A wagon clattered by, and a woman Sara recognized from church waved at her from atop the bench. It was so different living in a small town. In Boston she could have walked all day and never crossed paths with a familiar face.

She made her way past the post office to Parnell's Grocery. She had come here before with Hetty. It was much smaller than the grocery store she'd shopped at in Boston, but it stocked the necessities, and since it was the only store in town, it carried other items besides food: bolts of fabric, knitting supplies, trinkets. Most of the people around here grew their own food and stored it up to last the winter.

The bell over the door jangled when she entered, and Mr. Parnell looked up and gave her a nod. He was measuring sugar for another woman, so Sara browsed the selection of calico fabrics while she waited. There were other women in the store, but none Sara knew.

When Mr. Parnell was free to help her, she stepped up to the counter and requested five pounds of flour. She paid for her purchase and was turning to go when she heard the bell jingle, announcing someone's arrival.

"You have a pleasant day now, Mrs. McClain," Mr. Parnell called.

The silhouetted customer glided toward Sara, becoming more distinct with each step. When she had come close, her features were clear, and Sara saw it was that Mara Lawton. Eyes, in the iciest shade of blue, scanned Sara's frame with boredom.

Sara squirmed and shifted the bag of flour to the other arm.

"Hello, Sandra."

"Sara," she corrected automatically.

Mara went on as though uninterrupted. "Have you finished reading the book I gave you? Was Nate surprised I came to your shower?" she sneered.

Nate? "N–no. I mean, I guess not," Sara replied, confused.

Mara tipped her chin and raised a finely arched brow. "Well. I figured he may have thought it would be rather awkward for you. Under the circumstances."

"The circumstances?" Sara's brow furrowed.

"Oh. I don't suppose he's told you. We're quite close, you see. In fact, if my father had permitted it, *I* would have been the new Mrs. McClain."

Sara's face blanched, and she began to fidget with the ruffle on her dress.

The corner of Mara's pink mouth turned up in a smirk. "I was utterly shocked when he told me he was ordering a bride!"

Her voice had raised a notch, and Sara glanced furtively around to see if anyone had heard. There were some people in the store, several standing close enough to have heard. Heat rose to her cheeks.

Mara continued. "I mean, what kind of woman would market herself in such a way? Run off and marry a man she'd never set eyes on." She clicked her tongue and lowered her voice. "Of course, I could understand Nathan's predicament. A man his age wants to settle down and have children. It's unfortunate he couldn't have his first choice in a woman. Have no fear, though, we'll be discreet. . ."

The blood drained from Sara's face, and her lips worked silently for a moment until the words found their way out.

"I. . .I have to go. . ." She hastened through the door, the bell tinkling in laughter behind her.

The town swept by in a blur, and bile rose to her throat. She clutched her stomach with her free hand.

She was hateful, that woman! As ugly on the inside as she was pretty on the outside! How could Nathan like such a wretched woman, much less. . .

Oh! The horror of it! No wonder he resented her so! He couldn't have the woman he wanted, so he'd married *her!* Did everyone know? She'd never been so humiliated in all her life! Now she knew why Mara had seemed so unfriendly at the bridal shower. Sara had married the man she wanted for herself!

She was grateful for the long walk back and forced herself to slow her steps. It was going to take some time to sort through her thoughts.

Nathan had married her because he couldn't have Mara.

That knowledge shouldn't trouble her much. After all, she had married *him* to escape Pete. It did bother her, though. She was second choice, and he clearly resented her for it. In a way, they had each used the other. It was a sorry start for a marriage, but she could learn to live with it. If it weren't for that *other.*

Could it be true? Was he carrying on a. . .a liaison (she had never even uttered such a word) with that. . .that woman? It must be so. Why would she lie about such a thing?

It was a betrayal of the worst kind. Theirs may be an unconventional marriage, but she had the right to expect his faithfulness. . .didn't she? It's no wonder he didn't seek companionship with her. He'd already found it elsewhere!

Plainly, Hetty didn't know of this. She'd never condone such immorality. Was the rest of the town unaware also? It was humiliating enough to know it herself!

She was so inexperienced in such things that she didn't know what to do. She didn't dare confront Nathan about it—didn't even feel she had the right. It wasn't a true marriage. Oh, it was a real marriage in the eyes of the law, but she and Nathan knew better.

Confronting Mara was out of the question. Her haughty manner made Sara feel ugly and insignificant. Anyway, talking to Mara was not likely to do any good: She clearly had no qualms about her conduct. She'd even had the boldness to personally announce her wickedness to Sara! She'd never met such a brash woman. More than anything, she wished never to see Mara again, but that was unlikely, given the size of Cedar Springs.

It was a futile situation. She couldn't confront Nathan or Mara. She had no choice but to wait it out. Perhaps the embers would grow cold, given time. In the meantime, she could only hope that Nathan would have the consideration to exercise discretion.

She had rounded the bend that put the house in view. Blackie bounded out to greet her. In the four weeks she'd been there, the dog had filled out nicely.

Hetty was running clothes through the wringer when Sara and Blackie returned. "That's a long way to carry a bag of flour, ain't it?

"My arm's ready to fall off."

Sara passed her and started up the porch steps. Hetty's words stopped her.

"Somethin' wrong, Sara?"

She turned. "What makes you ask?"

"You look a little peaked, that's all. Somethin' happen in town?"

"No, I. . .I expect I'm just a little worn out from the walk."

"Mmm. That can happen. It's a good ways to town, and sometimes that sun beatin' down on ya can feel like fire on your skin."

"That must be it."

"Well, the house is good 'n' cool. Why don't ya go rest a spell."

"I think I'll do that, Hetty."

She put the flour on the kitchen shelf and went to her room. Some time alone to collect her thoughts was just what she needed.

෫෨

Later that afternoon, Sara wandered out to the stables. She wasn't in the frame of mind for human companionship, but horses, she'd found when she was just a little girl, are good company when one is troubled. They'd let you talk until you solved your problem, with nary a word of advice.

And if you weren't in the mood to talk, well, that was all right, too.

The stable was empty, save for a palomino, all the others having been put to pasture. Sara retrieved a currycomb and advanced slowly upon the mare so as not to spook her. Her front hoof was wrapped, giving evidence of a recent injury, but even so, the horse showed no signs of distress upon Sara's approach. Sara reached out and let the horse nuzzle her hand.

"Hello there, girl. What a beauty you are."

The mare's tan hide and ivory mane reminded Sara of the horse her mother had favored when they lived on the horse farm. Pepper. A smile lit her face when she remembered her mother's confusion over the name. "I can't imagine why they named such a fair-colored horse Pepper!" Later, they found out when they went off for a ride. It seemed Pepper was known for his frequent fits of sneezing. Sara and her mother had had a good laugh together. They had been so happy then. If only her father hadn't died.

Everything had spiraled downhill after that. They had to leave the farm, and her mother had to take in sewing to earn a meager living for the two of them. When things got quite bad, Sara offered to quit school and find a job, but her mother wouldn't hear of it. "No daughter of mine is going to be uneducated. School is important. We'll manage somehow."

And they had. Until her mother lost two of her regular customers.

It had seemed that Pete came along at just the right time. He'd been so kind and considerate, and Sara was glad to have someone taking a little of the burden off her mother. They'd had a whirlwind courtship, and when money grew impossibly tight, Pete offered to marry Sara's mother.

It was a move of desperation, Sara knew now. Her mother had not loved him, but had simply married him for security. It was ironic, really. The marriage had caused an upheaval in their lives the likes of which they'd never known. In her mind Pete was to blame, not only for his horrible treatment of her mother, but for the illness that robbed her young mother of life.

The horse nickered and tossed her head. "So you want some attention, do you?"

Sara pulled the metal-toothed comb through the horse's mane. If it weren't for her father, Sara would be tempted to think that all men were vermin. First Pete and now Nathan. How did she get herself into such a mess? More importantly, how would she get herself out?

ten

"How's your new wife workin' out?" Luke Reiley asked. He and Nathan were sitting on Luke's porch the next day, drinking lemonade and resting from a long afternoon in the sun.

"Fine, just fine."

"She's a little bit of a thing, ain't she? Saw ya standin' together in church. Reminded me of David 'n' Goliath!"

"It's about time for me to be getting back."

"Hetty said some awful nice things about her. You've really been blessed, Nathan. No tellin' what kinda woman you coulda got from that ad." Luke's face formed a wide grin, causing his one dimple to show.

Nathan's head whipped around. Luke was the closest thing he had to a best friend, but he hadn't told him about the ad. His eyes searched Luke's face. "Who told you that?"

"Mara Lawton." His eyes twinkled. "Is it true?"

Nathan's jaw set. "Where'd Mara hear a thing like that?"

"Didn't say. She's mighty jealous, though! I think she hoped to snag ya herself!"

"You know my feelings on *that*," Nathan said.

"Yeah, well, now it's my problem. Yesterday she started battin' those lashes at me and drapin' herself all over my arm!"

"Serves you right, after needling me about it all this time."

Luke laughed. "I s'pose you're right." His face sobered.

"Anyway, thought you'd wanna know what Mara told me. If she told me, I expect she's fixin' to tell anyone who'll stop to listen. Half the town prob'ly knows by now."

"Great." Nathan stood and handed his glass to Luke. "Gotta be going. It's getting close to suppertime."

"Thanks for the help today, Nate."

Nathan waved and mounted his stallion.

"Say, Nathan. . .I was just wonderin'. . .when ya order a bride, is she delivered all wrapped in parcel, or do ya have to go an' get her?"

Nathan scowled and nudged his horse to a walk.

"Aw, come on, Nate! I'm only joshin'!" Luke chortled and shook his head as he watched his surly friend ride away.

&

Nathan slammed the stall door shut, yanked off his hat, and flung it to the floor. He had a feeling he'd be better off skipping what was left of the evening.

First he'd found out about Mara's gossiping, then he'd endured Luke's badgering. How had Mara found out about the advertisement, anyhow? To top it off, Mr. Murphy's steers busted the fence again, and he'd spent the last hour rounding them up.

He was late for supper, and his rumbling stomach and foul mood gave evidence of his hunger. He marched to the house and entered, shutting the door with more force than he'd intended.

Sara, Hetty, and Gus were finishing their supper when Nathan came in. He closed the door with a bang, and Sara jumped.

As he stomped over to the table, Hetty fetched his plate from the black stove. "What's wrong, Nathan?"

"Mr. Murphy's steers busted through the fence again."

Gus lowered his fork. "Did ya get 'em back?"

"They're back. Didn't have time to fix the fence. I just strung some wire."

"We'll get to it tomorrow."

Hetty helped Sara clear the table while Nathan finished eating. Sara had insisted on taking over the cleanup duty after supper, so she shooed Hetty out of the kitchen.

When Sara returned to the table for more dishes, Hetty said, "Did ya know we got a birthday comin' up, Sara?"

"Whose?"

"Gus's. He's gonna be fifty on Tuesday!"

"Now, woman, why'd ya have to go an' bring that up for?"

"Well, I just thought we'd wanna make it right special— it bein' your fiftieth an' all."

Hetty talked of plans, while she and Gus prepared to leave. Nathan was still eating, his brooding silence betraying his foul mood.

Hetty turned just before she slipped out the door. "Oh! Sara—I been meanin' to ask ya when your birthday is. Wouldn't wanna skip right over it without knowin'!"

Sara turned from the basin. "It's not until July. The fifteenth."

"How old ya gonna be?"

"Twenty." As soon as she uttered the word, her eyes darted toward Nathan. His fork paused on his plate, and he slowly turned his head. His eyes pierced her, and she froze in place.

Hetty and Gus were saying good-bye, oblivious to the strained silence. The slam of the door was echoed as Nathan's fist came down on the table.

Sara jumped. Her muscles were taut with apprehension.

His chair grated across the floor, and her eyes swung to

his face. He wore a fearsome expression—his muscles tight and clenched. Angry brows formed a line over his squinty eyes.

He stood and rose to his full height. "You lied to me." His voice was low and scratchy. He advanced.

"I. . .I. . ." She shook her head and retreated. One step. Two steps. Three. Her body hit the wood wall with a thud. She was breathing rapidly, and her mouth was parched. Her lips moved vainly, the words not coming.

Her gaze was bolted to his, and she heard his feet shuffle to a stop—saw his arm fly up. . . She spun to the wall, cradling her head with an arm, cringing in anticipation of the coming blow.

Nathan stopped his arm in midair and watched in confusion as Sara huddled against the wall, her arm thrown up for. . .protection?

Dear God in heaven! She couldn't think. . . ? He heard a whimper and released the breath he held. All the rage he'd embraced just moments before gushed out of his body, replaced by something quite different.

He reached out a tentative hand and touched her raised arm. "Sara?"

He heard a pitiful squeak as she flinched and drew her body up tighter. He withdrew his hand.

"Sara, I'm sorry. . .I'd never. . .I just lost my temper. . ." He knew he wasn't making any sense. He'd never been good with words and never regretted it as much as now.

He reached out again and took her arm, this time determined to convince her that he was harmless. She fought, pushing at him and hitting him. He captured her flailing arms and pulled her to him. She struggled against him, but he put his arms around her, pinning her body to his. She continued to writhe, but he held her easily. Her chest heaved from her exertion, and he could feel her heart thumping like that of a hunted squirrel.

At some point she stopped fighting him, although she remained rigid in his arms. He talked to her, crooning gentle words, coaxing her to relax. Slowly, he loosened his hold on her and stroked her back with awkward hands.

Later he wouldn't remember what he'd said, but it had the desired effect. Before long, Sara hung limp in his arms, spent from her efforts.

Nathan released her and held her away from him. Her eyes were closed, and there were traces of tears on her cheeks. Never had he felt like such a savage! He'd scared her to the point of fearing he would hurt her. His hands looked huge against her tiny shoulders and he felt ashamed.

"Sara?"

She felt Nathan's knuckle on her chin, tipping it up, and she opened her eyes to meet his. Confusion was reflected in their gray depths. Her eyes fell to a small stain on his shirt, as color suffused her face. Her lip trembled, and she bit down in order to still it.

Nathan drew a handkerchief from his pocket and dried her face, his strong hands gentle in their task. She blinked, and another tear was released.

"You keep that up and I'm gonna be here all night," he said.

He finished his ministrations and guided her to the settee, seating himself beside her. There was a fire to ward off the chill during the night, and its orange flames licked the logs.

Nathan turned toward her. "Do you want to talk about it? About who did this to you?"

She fingered the folds in her dress. "I—it was my stepfather. . .Pete."

Nathan looked at the fire and seemed to be weighing this piece of information. "And your mother?"

"She died. . .last year."

"What about before? Did he hit her, too?"

"Yes." It was spoken so softly, she wondered if he heard her. She cleared her throat. "He. . .he never hit me until she died. He drank. . . It made him crazy." Her eyes filled with tears, and the fire blurred into a hazy image.

"Do you have any brothers or sisters?"

"No. . . It was just me after Mama died. Just me and Pete." A tear spilled over her lashes and traveled down her cheek. Sara kept her eyes in her lap, but she felt Nathan's gaze on her, studying her profile. The popping of the fire seemed unnaturally loud.

Nathan drew in a long breath and exhaled loudly. She wondered what he was thinking and she was tempted to meet his gaze, but she couldn't. She was embarrassed. Ashamed.

"That's the reason you married me."

At these words, her eyes swung to his. His face was void of expression. She opened her mouth to speak but shut it again when she thought of nothing to say.

"You answered my ad, hoping to get away from your stepfather." It was a statement, not a question.

Her lips trembled. "Yes." She watched her hand as it traced the piping on the edge of the cushion.

She didn't know what she expected next: anger, disappointment, something. But he surprised her again.

His large, rough hand covered hers. "It's okay."

She stared at their hands, his so dark next to hers, and fought the emotion that welled up in her.

"I'm glad I could offer you a way out. I'm glad you're not with him anymore."

Their eyes melded and, for the first time, she saw kindness in them. When he withdrew his hand and looked away, she realized he was as uncomfortable as she was.

Sara suddenly realized how weary she was, and her shoulders slumped. She remembered the dishes soaking in the basin, but she didn't have the energy to do them.

"I–I think I'll turn in now." She pulled herself up to standing.

Nathan rose, too. "Good night, Sara."

"Good night."

She walked to the stairs and started up. On the third step she heard him call her name and turned to look over her shoulder. "Yes?"

Nathan stood by the settee, his hands in his pockets. "You're safe here. I just wanted you to know."

Sara nodded once, then turned quickly and climbed the stairs. She didn't want him to see the tears that had gathered in her eyes again.

eleven

A bird's tune roused Sara from a deep sleep. Her lids felt puffy and swollen as she cracked them open. Then she remembered—the lie. . .the fear. . .the crying. Nathan had been so gentle with her. She'd never thought him capable of such tenderness. She snuggled deeper into the covers, relishing for a moment the feelings that washed over her. How wonderful it had felt to be held and comforted by a man! It felt so different than when her mama or Helen had held her. So delightfully different!

Sara noticed the light flooding through the window. Hetty would be well into breakfast preparations by now, and she'd left the supper dishes in the basin! She dressed quickly in her calico dress and scurried downstairs.

Sure enough, Hetty was flipping pancakes and the table was set. The basin, however, was empty.

"Good morning, Hetty. Sorry to be late." Sara tied on an apron.

"No trouble at all, Sara. It's just pancakes and bacon this mornin'."

"Thank you for doing the dishes. I intended to do them before you came, but I overslept."

"What dishes are you talkin' about, dear?"

"Why, the supper dishes. The ones I left in the basin last night."

"There were no dishes there when I came in." Hetty turned the sizzling bacon.

Sara frowned. If Hetty hadn't done them, who had. . . ?

Oh, surely not! She had never in all her life seen a man wash dishes! But, it must have been him—there was no one else. Who was this man she'd married?

Sara pulled herself out of her stupor. She had to help get breakfast on the table before the men finished their morning chores.

Gus came in shortly after, followed by Nathan.

"Good mornin', ladies," Gus said. Sara and Hetty returned his greeting.

Nathan took off his hat and tossed it on a chair. "Morning, Hetty. Sara."

Sara's face flushed. "Good morning." Hetty watched the exchange and cocked a brow.

During the meal, conversation flowed in a newly relaxed manner. Even Sara took part in the discourse. Nathan was treating her with kindness, and she was beginning to see him in a new light. Breakfast passed quickly, and the men set out for the south pasture.

Sara and Hetty began some rigorous housework. The carpets on the floor were overdue for a good beating. Dust was caked in the crevices of all the carpets, a result of the dry spring. The work was exhausting, and Sara's back and arms ached by midmorning. Next, they worked on Gus and Hetty's featherbed, which had developed an odor. Together they emptied the feathers and washed them in a tub of suds.

Sara had been waiting all day for Hetty to ask about Nathan. She was a perceptive woman and had no doubt noticed the absence of tension at the breakfast table. The feathers were spread to dry before she broached the subject.

"I couldn't help but notice a change in you an' Nathan this mornin'. You two gettin' on better?"

Sara wiped the perspiration from her brow. "I guess you

could say we came to an understanding." She paused and Hetty remained silent, waiting for her to finish. "I've been very. . .cautious around Nathan. I guess I was afraid of him."

"Why is that, Sara? Oh, I know he's been gruff around ya, but he's a kind man. He certainly wouldn't hurt ya." They made their way in to the kitchen.

"I know that now. We worked it out." Sara poured them each a glass of lemonade and sank onto a chair. "You've never asked me why I answered Nathan's ad."

"Well, I didn't figure it was any of my business. A woman has her reasons."

"I did have my reasons, Hetty, but they weren't the usual ones." She tipped her glass up. "I needed to get away from Boston. My mama died last year, and there was just me and my stepfather. He was. . .well, he wasn't a kind man. He was a drinker, and he got terribly mean when he drank."

"Did he hurt you, Sara?"

"Yes," she whispered. "Not until my mama died, though. When she was alive, he took all his anger out on her. I could hear it from my room. . .the sound of him hitting her. It was dreadful; I was helpless to do anything. You know, Hetty, that was worse than getting hit myself. I tried to talk Mama into leaving, but she was afraid he'd find us, and we had no money to go away someplace. After she died, I took a job. Pete used most of my wages for drinking money, but I hid some away. I was planning to go someplace far away when I had saved enough. Then my friend, Helen, showed me Nathan's ad."

"Praise be to God. He sure was lookin' out for ya."

Sara was dazed for a moment. She'd never once considered God in all this. It was good fortune, she'd thought, that Helen had found the ad—just chance. Hetty had given her something to think on.

Sara looked at Hetty. "I'm just so glad I'm not there. Boston is miles away, and he can't hurt me anymore."

Hetty covered Sara's hand. "You were afraid Nathan was cut from the same cloth?"

"He seemed so cross with me all the time. And he's so big! Why, when I saw him at the depot, I wanted to scramble back on that train and head anyplace else!"

Hetty laughed, then covered her mouth. "I'm sorry, dear! I know it's not funny, but knowin' Nathan like I do, I can imagine how he scared ya out of your wits! He is a big man, and he was in a fine temper that day." Her face grew serious. "He really is harmless, ya know."

"I know that now."

"You sure went through a nasty time. It'd be hard to get over somethin' like that. Have ya forgiven him yet?"

"Forgiven him? He doesn't deserve it!" Sara watched Hetty's startled face. "Well, he doesn't! He's not even sorry! His actions were mean and deliberate. Even if I could forgive him for what he did to me, I could never forgive him for what he did to Mama."

"I'm sorry, dear. That must be quite a burden to carry around." Hetty took their glasses to the kitchen. "Well, we got a garden that's finally ready for plantin', and it's not gonna plant itself! I'm just itchin' to get started!"

"I'm afraid you've got a greenhorn on your hands," Sara said.

"There's not much to it. You'll see."

Sara and Hetty labored in the garden for the rest of the afternoon. Sara found that she liked the feel of the earth between her fingers. The ground was a little dry from lack of rain, but when they dug little holes for the seeds, they found dark, moist dirt.

It was to be a large garden, located behind the main

house. By the end of the afternoon they had planted only one-quarter of it. Sara knew it was going to be a lot of work, but it was something she enjoyed. Besides, they would have vegetables all winter! Peas, onions, potatoes. She could hardly wait to taste them! Hetty seemed concerned that they were getting a late start on the garden, and she hoped the plants would grow in time for harvest, before the cold weather set in.

Back in Boston there had been no room for a garden, so they bought their produce at the market. They'd never had much produce through the winter, though, since it was so expensive.

When it was nearly suppertime, they washed up and prepared the meal. The men were in fine spirits that evening. They'd had a productive day, and they made quick work of the meal. It was rewarding to cook for men who appreciated their efforts. Pete had only complained about the meals she had prepared. Hetty talked about starting the garden, her face alight with excitement. Gardening was a chore that would get done without complaint.

They had such pleasant conversation that Sara was sorry to see Hetty and Gus go after supper. She considered asking them to stay but didn't want to intrude on their private time.

Sara washed the dishes and wondered about the rest of the evening. Would Nathan avoid her as he had been doing, or would there be a change in their routine? She decided she'd work on her needlepoint in the main room. If Nathan wanted to stay, he would.

She sat on the settee and threaded the needle. Blackie laid across her shoes, heaved a sigh, and closed his eyes.

She heard the plodding of Nathan's stocking feet as he made his way down the stairs. He shuffled to a stop at the bottom, and Sara continued her needlework, wondering what he'd do. Although the awful tension was gone, a new awkwardness brewed between them. She heard his footsteps as he entered the room, then watched as he took a seat in what she now thought of as "his chair."

He looked rather uncomfortable as he opened his book and began to study it. Sara looked down at it, too; it was upside down.

She continued working her needle, waiting for him to turn his book over. After a moment, she glanced up. It was still upside down, but his brows were drawn together in concentration, as if he were absorbing every word.

A grin tugged at her lips as she pushed the needle through the fabric. What on earth must he be thinking to be so unaware of his actions?

Sara decided to break the silence. "Is it a good book?"

"Huh? Oh—yeah, it's all right."

Sara determined to just come right out with it. "Um, Nathan?"

"Hmm?"

"Your book. It's upside down."

Nathan looked at her with a baffled expression, then looked down at his book. For the first time Sara saw redness creep up his neck. He looked sheepish as he flipped his book over. As she watched him, an irrepressible grin formed on his face. His eyes met hers, and she smiled in return.

"Guess I looked pretty silly, sitting here reading upside down."

"No. . .you just looked like someone with a lot on his mind."

He took a deep breath and let it out. "After last night. . . Well, I guess I'm just not sure how to go from here."

With the mention of the previous night, Sara was reminded

of the supper dishes he'd washed. "Oh! I wanted to thank you. . .for washing the dishes. You really shouldn't have. I was going to do them first thing this morning."

"I didn't mind. You had a rough night." He closed his book and laid it on the table. "There is something that I wanted to talk to you about." Leaning forward, he rested his elbows on his knees and stared at his hands. "You were honest with me last night. . .about why you married me, I mean." He looked at her then. "I think it's only fair to tell you why I placed that ad."

Sara felt her stomach tighten into a knot. Was he going to explain about Mara? Tell her she'd been his second choice? She waited for him to continue, but he seemed to be struggling for a way to begin. Finally, he drew a breath and started.

"My mother and father had a very special relationship. She died when I was born, so I never knew her, but my father. . .well, he never forgot her, never stopped loving her. He told me so many stories about her, sometimes I forgot that I didn't know her. When he'd talk about her, his face would come alive. I don't think he ever stopped missing her. . .grieving for her. He was always after me to find a woman and settle down. I suppose he wanted me to have what he and my mother had."

Sara laid her needlework aside and stroked Blackie's fur.

"Anyway, he got real sick a couple of months before he died. Doc Hathaway said there was nothing he could do for him. It just got worse and worse. In the end we were praying for God to take him home. He was in so much pain. When he did die, well. . .it was almost a relief. The suffering was over.

"A few days after he died, an attorney from Wichita came and brought my father's will with him. I didn't even know he had a will. The attorney explained that my father had asked him to make out the will when he'd first become ill. The will said that I would inherit the ranch, but if I didn't get married within one year, I'd have to sell it."

Sara's mouth fell open. He'd had to get married in order to keep his ranch?

"This ranch has been in my family for three generations. It's all I've known, and I wasn't about to give it up. I can't imagine why my father felt he had to do that. He wasn't one to strong-arm a person. I guess it just meant that much to him that I marry. Anyway, I put the ad in the paper in Boston, and you know the rest of the story. I've never told anyone about the will. Not even Hetty and Gus."

"Why Boston? I mean, Wichita is a good-sized city, and it's much closer."

"I did consider Wichita, and some other cities as well. It was a matter I prayed over for some time. In the end, I felt Boston was the right city."

Sara studied her folded hands. Was Hetty right, then? Had God played a part in all this? It seemed so farfetched that God would even have time to meddle with her life. The distant God she believed in would not be inclined to intervene on her behalf, or anyone else's for that matter. Hetty and Nathan plainly believed in a different kind of God.

Another thought, this one completely different, came to her mind. If he'd been forced into marriage, he must have considered Mara first. He must have asked her to be his wife, and that's when her father had denied him permission.

It was a humbling thought. Not only was she a distant second choice, but he hadn't even wanted a marriage to begin with. She felt as if she had imposed on his life—like she'd been foisted upon him. Her stomach churned with regret.

Her thoughts must have been reflected on her face, for his next words were spoken softly. "I'm sorry if this is. . . disappointing to you. I felt it best to be honest in this. If it makes you feel any better, I got quite a few letters in answer to my ad, but as soon as I got yours, I knew you were the one."

That did make Sara feel a trifle better. "Thank you. . .for telling me."

Darkness was descending upon the room, its only light being the fire. Sara stifled a yawn. Even if she was of a mind to continue her needlepoint, it was getting too dark. "I think I'll turn in now." She stood, and he copied the movement.

"Good night, Sara."

"Good night."

After going to her room, she let down her hair and changed into her white nightie. She settled herself under the quilt and tried to quiet the ceaseless activity in her mind.

❧

Sara bolted upright and sat with her ears alert and her heart thrashing in her chest. She'd heard a sound. A bump, she thought, but she couldn't be certain, for she'd been sleeping soundly and had heard it on the rim of her consciousness.

She scanned the room and relaxed when she saw where she was. This wasn't her room in Boston, and Pete wasn't going to come crashing through the door. She was at the ranch in Kansas. Safe.

She fell back against her pillow and willed her heart to slow its pace. When would she get beyond the horror of her life in Boston?

The room was nearly pitch-black, so she knew the night was well under way. She turned over and closed her eyes in an attempt to coax her body back to sleep. After several minutes, it became clear that she was too restless to fall asleep again.

A yearning for a cool glass of water sent her padding across the wood floor. She tiptoed down the staircase, feeling her way as she went, rounded the corner, and passed the table.

"Couldn't sleep?"

Sara jumped with a start, her hand flying to her chest. "Oh! Nathan! I think you scared ten years off my life!" She grasped the back of an empty chair.

"Sorry. Didn't mean to startle you."

He was sitting in the dark, and she could just make out his form. He stood and walked to the wall lamp. "Let me light this so you can see where you're going."

As he lit the lamp, she went into the kitchen and called to him. "I'm pouring myself a glass of water; would you like some?"

"No, thanks. I already have some." His chair groaned as he seated himself.

She pumped water into a glass and had just started for the dining room when he spoke.

"I think I'll head back up to. . ."

He stopped when Sara came into the doorway. He was studying her in an odd way that made her aware of the nightgown she was wearing. It was modest, and showed less of her than a dress, but a nightie seemed so intimate. She wrapped her arms around herself.

"What?" she asked.

"Your hair."

A hand fluttered to her hair, and she realized it was down. Her heart sank when she remembered all the disparaging remarks Pete had made about it. Her eyes found the floor.

She blurted out, "I know it's. . .it's. . ."

"Lovely."

Her startled eyes met his. "All those curls. I had no idea. And it falls clear to your waist."

Her face heated and she took a sip of water to cover her embarrassment.

"You should wear it down all the time. It's very becoming."

She rewarded him with a timid smile. "That wouldn't be very proper. . .or practical."

He smiled in return. "No, I suppose it wouldn't," he said. "Well, as I was saying, I think I'll head back up to my room. 'Night."

"Good night."

She stood staring at the staircase long after he was gone.

twelve

The end of the next day found Nathan riding in from the northern pasture. The horse was trotting at an unhurried pace, his hooves stirring up dust from the parched ground. It had been a dry spring, and the hot days of summer stretched ahead like an endless abandoned road. Already the grass was beginning to dry to a withered brown, leaving the cattle to graze in the lowlands where the ground was more fertile.

A dry summer could cause many hardships for the ranchers and farmers, especially after the bitter winter of '86. A series of blizzards had wiped out many cattle and brought low prices for the scrawny animals that had survived.

Nathan said a quick prayer for rain and thanked God that they had been able to put up hay to feed their cattle.

He saw his house on the horizon and pulled back on the reins to slow his mount. For some reason he wasn't eager to get home. The horse plodded along, giving Nathan time to examine his feelings. If he were honest with himself, he would admit that Sara was the reason for his reluctance.

Sara.

She was slipping into his heart, and he knew it. When he had seen her last night, with her hair spilling around her shoulders, he'd wanted to run his fingers through the soft curls. She was so beautiful and so completely unaware of it! That was the truly amazing part. Most of the women he knew used their looks for their own benefit. But not Sara.

Her vulnerability ate at his defenses, gnawing away a little at a time. He felt helpless to stop the new sensations she was causing.

He'd have to do a better job of guarding his heart if he hoped to remain unfettered by deep feelings for his new wife. What was wrong with him, anyway, that he couldn't stick to his simple plan? He'd thought he had more discipline than this.

He dismounted and led his horse into the stable as Sara rounded the side of the house, carrying two empty buckets.

≈

Sara raised her free hand in a wave to Nathan, and he returned the greeting. Hetty was in the kitchen getting supper ready, and Sara was finishing up the garden work. They had finished planting, and she was using buckets of water to wet the newly buried seeds. She hoped the dry weather wouldn't ruin all their hard work.

Her back and shoulders ached as she pumped water into the large buckets. She'd made many trips already and had determined that this would be her last for today. Nathan was back, so Gus wouldn't be far behind. She needed to help Hetty get supper on the table.

After filling the other bucket, she stooped over and hoisted them off the ground. She had staggered no more than half a dozen steps when she heard Nathan approaching from behind.

"What do you think you're doing?" he demanded.

Sara turned quickly, and some water sloshed on her shoes. Her task had caused her breathing to be labored, so she gasped in reply, "I–I'm just taking some water to the garden."

"Do you have any notion what those buckets weigh?

You're gonna break your back. Now, put 'em down!" His tone left no room for argument, so she eased them to the ground. "You're too frail for this kind of work. Just go on in the house and tend to supper."

Tears gathered in her eyes and she spun away and darted toward the house before he could see them. She cursed her shapeless body all the way. "Scrawny," Pete had called it. Frail, scrawny, it was all the same—hers was not a body a man would admire. That realization had never bothered her much before. All the names Pete had ever called her hadn't hurt as much as now hearing Nathan insult her. She stopped suddenly on the porch as understanding surfaced.

It hurt because she cared about Nathan. He had a power over her that Pete never had.

She looked back toward the pump and saw that he had disappeared, along with the buckets. The garden was getting its water after all. Well, that was just fine. Let Mr. Tough and Mighty do the work himself! What was he all about, anyway? Kind one day, mean the next. He should just make up his mind and stick with it!

Sara used her sleeve to wipe away any trace of tears, straightened her shoulders, and went in the house to help Hetty.

ò

The following Sunday, Sara found herself the object of some curious glances. She discreetly checked the buttons on her rust-colored dress, but found them all securely in their buttonholes.

After they took their seats in the pew, Sara tried to put it from her mind. Everyone stood when Luke came forward to lead the music. Sara was familiar with the song, so she sang along. The congregation seated itself following the hymn, and Reverend Hill took the podium.

"Two weeks ago I spoke to you about sin—how all of us have it, no matter our age or religion. None of us is perfect. I've felt God leading me to do a continuation of that sermon, and today I'd like to explain how the grace of God frees us from sin. To many of you this will be a repeat of what you've heard many times before, but for some of you, this may be life-changing news.

"If I were to stand here today and talk only of our sin—if that were the end of the story—we'd all be doomed to hell. Deserving of it, even. Romans 6:23 says, 'For the wages of sin is death; but the gift of God is eternal life through Jesus Christ our Lord.' The wages of sin is *death*. That's spiritual death, dear friends. Hell. As I said, if the story ended there, there would be no hope. But the verse goes on. The second part says, 'but the gift of God is eternal life through Jesus Christ our Lord.' What is this gift that Paul writes of? How do we get eternal life through Jesus Christ? Let's turn to Romans 5:8."

Sara flipped through the pages of her Bible trying to find Romans. This is what she'd asked Hetty about. She was finally going to get her answers.

Hetty reached over and helped her find the reference just as Reverend Hill began to read.

" 'But God commendeth his love toward us, in that, while we were yet sinners, Christ died for us.' God's gift was His Son, Jesus Christ. Even though we were sinners, He died a cruel death on the cross in our place. Our sins required a perfect sacrifice. And Jesus was that sacrifice. He laid down His life so that we might have eternal life."

Sara stared at Reverend Hill in wonder. Never before had she heard this story! Jesus was not some historical figure. He was God's very own Son! And He had died for her!

Reverend Hill continued. "You may be asking yourself what you must do to obtain this eternal life. Do you have to work for it? Do you have to die for it? No, friends. It's a gift. All you have to do is receive it. God made this simple so that even someone as dim-witted as I am can understand it!"

He smiled as a ripple of laughter fanned the congregation.

"Being saved is easy. Jesus already did the hard part. All we need to do is ask forgiveness for our sins and believe that Jesus died to cover our sins. Then, by the grace of God, our sins are covered. The Bible says in Isaiah 1:18, 'though your sins be as scarlet, they shall be as white as snow.' If you haven't received God's generous gift, I invite you to do so now. Let us pray."

The reverend prayed, but Sara didn't hear the words. She was too busy talking to God. *Oh, Lord, I've been so wrong about You! You're not the distant, uncaring God I thought You were! Thank You for loving me enough to give Your Son as a sacrifice for my sins. I'm sorry for my sins, which made His dying necessary. I accept Your gift, Father. Amen.*

Sara blotted away a tear with her sleeve. She was glad that the reverend was still praying, for it gave her a moment to compose herself.

When the prayer ended, Sara gathered her belongings. Everything was the same, yet she felt so different. Even the inquiring glances did nothing to diminish her spirits. She was excited and longed to tell Hetty of her experience. That would have to keep until tomorrow, though, for she wanted to tell her in private.

❧

As it turned out, Hetty was feeling under the weather the next morning. She came to prepare breakfast as usual, but when Sara heard her scratchy "Good mornin' " and saw her glassy eyes, Sara felt her forehead. Hetty was sent back home with an admonition to stay in bed and rest. Hetty argued halfheartedly, then gave in.

Sara was determined to take good care of Hetty while she was sick. Hetty had been so good to her, and she wanted to repay her in some way.

Tuesday arrived, and Hetty was still sick. It was Gus's birthday, and Hetty was dismayed that she wasn't able to make his cake, but Sara was happy to do it. They took the party to Hetty's room that night and had a splendid time, despite Hetty's illness.

Hetty had already bought Gus's present: a brown suede hat with a tan sweatband encircling it. His old hat was worn and frayed.

"This looks too nice to work in, darlin'!"

"Nonsense. That's what it's for!"

Sara had picked out a belt buckle, with Hetty's help. She could tell by Nathan's expression that he approved.

The week was a busy one for Sara. Between her usual chores and caring for Hetty, she was worn ragged by the end of the week.

Hetty was feeling better by Friday, although still weak. When Sara brought Hetty lunch, she decided to ask her a question that had been on her mind all week.

"Hetty, did you notice anything unusual at Sunday services?"

"Unusual? I'm not sure I know what you mean."

"Well, it seemed to me that people were looking at me

kind of funny. I'd understand if this were my first service, but it's not, and I was wondering if you might know what's going on."

Hetty smoothed the frayed edge of the quilt. "I've been frettin' over whether or not to tell you, Sara, but I think you have a right to know. Somehow, folks around here found out about how you and Nathan met."

Sara drew in a sharp breath.

"Now, it's not all that bad. A couple of the womenfolk made mention of it to me. They were very kind and just wanted me to let you know. Nobody is thinkin' bad things about you, if that's what you're worryin' about. This town is filled with good people, and I don't think you're givin' 'em enough credit," she said gently.

"Come to think of it, the people who were looking at me looked more curious than anything. You're probably right." Still, Sara couldn't help but feel embarrassed and a little humiliated.

"Of course I'm right. I'm sure they'll forget all about it before you know it."

On Saturday, Hetty announced she was fit as a fiddle and would not be kept in bed another day. And so, after breakfast, Sara and Hetty set off for town to buy some food and supplies.

The warm air betrayed the coming of summer. The sky was clear blue and the fresh air was still. Unseen birds were twittering, their songs mingling with the clattering of the wagon.

They'd ridden no more than a mile when Sara decided she couldn't keep her news any longer.

"Hetty, there's something I've been wanting to share with you all week, but there really hasn't been a proper time."

"What is it?"

"I'm afraid I owe you an apology."

Hetty looked up from the road. "Whatever for?"

"When I came here, I led you—well, all of you, really—to believe I was a Christian. I wasn't, Hetty. And I'm sorry that I deceived you."

"I know that, dear." Sara shot her an astonished look. "Well, I couldn't *know*. Only you and the Lord can know for sure. But I did suspect."

"Why?"

"Some of the questions you asked. Things you said. Things you didn't say. I notice you said you *weren't* a Christian. Does this mean what I think?"

"Yes! Just this past Sunday I accepted God's gift. I never understood before. I'd heard the story of Jesus, of course, but I thought He was just a man who'd been put to death. And I believed in God, but I thought He just existed, separate from us. It never connected before. But Sunday, during Reverend Hill's sermon, the pieces just fell into place, and I saw it all so clearly. Like a completed puzzle."

"I'm so delighted for you!" Hetty reached over to embrace Sara, tugging the reins to the right as she did. They held each other for a moment and then sprung apart when the wagon ran off the road. Hetty guided the horses back onto the road. When all was settled, the women looked at each other and burst into gales of laughter.

≈

All week long Sara had been turning in after supper, exhausted from the additional chores and her care of Hetty. Therefore, Saturday night after supper, Sara found herself alone with Nathan for the first time all week.

While she'd been excited about sharing her news with

Hetty, she was a little anxious about doing the same with Nathan. She didn't know how he'd feel about being lied to. It was his ad, after all, and she distinctly remembered referring to herself as a Christian in one of her letters. He wasn't likely to take it as lightly as Hetty had. Besides, she never knew from one day to the next what kind of mood he was in.

And so, it was with some trepidation that she rested her book on her lap and began speaking. "Nathan, there's something I've been wanting to tell you."

He had stopped what he was doing, and it was at just that moment that she realized he was cleaning his gun. She derisively thought how poor her timing was!

He was waiting for her to continue.

"There was something in my letters to you that was untruthful," she said.

He studied her for a moment. "I know. . .your age. We already laid that to rest."

Sara colored and looked at her book. It was bad enough to have the one lie to confess, but now she was reminded that it wasn't the only one she'd told! "No. . .no. Not that."

"There's more?" His eyebrows disappeared under his bangs.

Sara flushed a deeper red. "I–I'm afraid there is. Although this untruth has already been resolved. I mean, it was an untruth, but now it's not, and—"

"What on earth are you talking about?"

"I said I was a Christian," she blurted.

Nathan looked totally confused now. "You said you were a Christian. . ." Understanding dawned. ". . .and you're not?"

"I wasn't."

Nathan shook his head, as if to clear it.

She tried again. "I wrote that I was a Christian, and I wasn't. However, just this past Sunday, I became a believer."

Sara gave Nathan a moment to digest this. He leaned back in his chair, his hands folded on his chest. "I'm real glad about your decision."

"I know I shouldn't have lied. I'm sorry. I was so anxious to get away—desperate, really. I know that's no excuse."

"I understand, Sara. It was wrong of you, but I do understand why you did it."

"Thank you, Nathan."

"If you'd told me about this before you'd accepted Christ, I'm afraid I wouldn't have been so understanding."

"Yes. I know you wanted a wife who shared your beliefs."

"It's much more than that, Sara. In 2 Corinthians 6:14 it says, 'Be ye not unequally yoked together with unbelievers.' That means it's a sin for a Christian to marry an unbeliever."

Sara was taken back. "You mean it was a sin for me to marry you? And I caused you to sin as well?"

"Since you didn't know what the Bible has to say about the subject, I don't reckon you can be held accountable for that. As far as I'm concerned, I wasn't aware you were an unbeliever. The important thing is that you're a Christian now."

"There's so much I don't know. I feel like a child discovering a whole new world."

"You'll find the answers you need in that Bible of yours. I'm here, too. And Hetty and Gus. But I think you'll learn most by studying God's Word."

"I've been meaning to start reading all week, but I've been so worn out by suppertime. Maybe mornings would be a better time."

"I was meaning to tell you. You did a fine job of caring for things all by yourself this week. Your cooking's as good as Hetty's."

Her face heated at the compliment. "Thank you."

Nathan quickly busied himself with his gun. If she didn't know better, she'd think he was a little flustered himself.

thirteen

Sara had looked forward to her first Sunday service as a Christian. She knew her hunger for knowledge would be quenched by Reverend Hill's teaching. Pretending to be a Christian had been harder than she had imagined, and she was relieved to discontinue the pretense.

The day was overcast, and the gray clouds gave everyone renewed hope for some much-needed rain.

Sara and Hetty alighted from the carriage with the help of their husbands. They were a bit early, as usual, and small groups of people mingled, sharing news of the week and speculations on the weather. It was from one such group that Mara Lawton emerged.

Sara halted in her tracks, surprised to see the woman at church, then continued only when Hetty treaded on her heels.

Sara hadn't seen Mara since that horrible scene at the grocer's, but a meeting was unavoidable now. Sara didn't know whether Nathan's presence made her feel protected or more vulnerable. Would Mara say something to embarrass her in front of her new husband?

Mara approached wearing a frost-blue dress that matched her eyes perfectly. It was embellished with lace and ribbon and hung upon her curvy figure in a most enticing way. The collar scooped low on her neck in an almost risqué display of skin.

She's not bashful about her figure, that's for certain. And in church, no less! Sara thought.

Hetty and Gus went their own direction when they saw a

group of friends, so Sara and Nathan were alone when Mara drew near.

"Hello, Nathan," said Mara, her voice syrupy.

"Mara." Nathan tipped his hat. "Have you met my wife Sara?"

Mara's cold eyes bore into Sara's. "Yes, I attended her bridal shower. Hello again, Sara."

"Hello," she whispered. Her face heated as she remembered the humiliating blow she'd been dealt that day at the grocer's shop. If she was worried about what Mara would say to her today, her fears were unfounded. After the brief hello, Mara ignored her completely.

Nathan and Mara continued to exchange words but Sara didn't hear them. She just stood, shifting her weight from one foot to the other. Nathan was her husband, but at that moment, Sara felt like an intruder.

Just when she thought she couldn't take it another moment, Nathan and Mara said their farewells. Nathan guided Sara into the church with a hand to her back, and seated her in their pew.

Sara felt her day had been ruined. She'd never forgotten what Mara told her at the grocery that day, but she had put it from her mind. Now she remembered it with a greater degree of anguish. She now knew Nathan much better than she had then, and the feelings that were growing in her heart made Mara's revelation hurt more than ever. Before, it had felt as if she had been betrayed by a stranger, but now her relationship with Nathan was much closer.

Hetty and Gus joined them, and the service soon began. Whenever Sara found her mind wandering, she prayed that God would help keep her mind from straying. When the sermon was over, she realized she had absorbed most of Reverend Hill's message.

Somehow, during that hour her mood had improved. Laura came over to visit with her, as did Mrs. Hill. Sara was the last one to exit the church, and the reverend was waiting at the door to greet her.

"Well, Mrs. McClain, you're looking in fine spirits this morning."

"Thank you, Reverend Hill. I also wanted to thank you for your sermon last Sunday. It cleared up many questions I had, and I'm pleased to say I accepted God's gift."

The reverend's smile widened. "I'm so happy to hear that, Sara! There's nothing that pleases me more than hearing that one of my flock has found the way home!"

Sara noticed that Hetty, Gus, and Nathan were waiting for her and said a quick good-bye to the preacher.

As she strode to the carriage, Sara resolved to put Mara from her mind. She'd entered this marriage with no guarantees for happiness, but finally things were beginning to look promising for Nathan and her. If nothing else, they were becoming friends, and that was a start. Perhaps if she continued trying to build their relationship, this thing with Mara would end.

❧

That evening Sara studied the Bible in her room. She found that she could concentrate better when she was alone.

She began in the eighteenth chapter of Matthew, from which Reverend Hill had preached that morning. He had focused on the third verse, and Sara wanted to continue from there. At the end of verse twenty-two she stopped and reread the last two verses, certain she'd misinterpreted them.

"Then Peter came to him, and said, 'Lord, how oft shall my brother sin against me, and I forgive him? till seven times?' Jesus said unto him, 'I say not unto thee, Until seven times: but, Until seventy times seven.' "

What did this mean? She read the rest of the chapter. It was about a servant who was indebted to his lord. The lord had compassion on him and released him from the debt. That same servant then went to a fellow servant who owed him money, but he had no compassion on his fellow servant and sent him to prison. When the first servant's lord heard of this, he sent the servant to the "tormentors" until his debt was paid. "So likewise shall my heavenly Father do also unto you, if ye from your hearts forgive not every one his brother their trespasses."

Sara's heart was troubled when she read the last verse. The words were clear, but she struggled to believe that they applied to her.

She reasoned that she shouldn't have to forgive Pete because she'd done nothing wrong, as the servant had. Pete's violence against her and her mother had been unprovoked.

Still, her eyes returned to the last verse, and she prayed earnestly that God would give her wisdom concerning these things.

❦

She was someplace dark and musty. The cellar, she thought. Her body trembled, her breathing was rapid. The footsteps drew closer, getting louder and louder. She cringed deeper into the hole and screamed when the door was flung open. Arms and legs thrashed about, tangled in a web of conflict. She cried out again and again, but it was futile. When he seized her arms, trapping her, her panic heightened. He was calling her name, but her eyes were squeezed tight, shutting off that horrible face.

"No! No!" she gasped.

"Sara!" He shook her hard and she opened her eyes.

His dark form loomed over her, and she resumed her struggle with new energy.

"Sara! Look at me!" He pinned her legs with one of his own, and she lay breathless, imprisoned by his body.

"Look at me! It's Nathan. Nathan."

The room was dim, but the filmy moonlight illuminated one side of his face.

"Nathan?" It was a desperate whisper.

"Yes." He released her and eased down onto the mattress beside her.

She sat up and clung to him, overcome with relief. His robe smelled of him, and she inhaled the masculine fragrance, letting it calm her. He stroked her back, soothing away the ugly memories. She felt safe, so safe, in Nathan's arms. Sometime later exhaustion set in, and her eyes drifted shut against the broad expanse of Nathan's chest.

≈

Nathan had heard her screams from his room and had come running. He hadn't hesitated at her door but had thrown it open, ready to encounter an intruder. All he'd found, though, was Sara, writhing in her bed, fighting an imaginary foe. He had realized during the course of their battle that her nightmare must have involved her stepfather.

It had taken some time to bring her around, but when she'd clutched onto him like she had, he'd longed to comfort her and make her feel safe.

Now, as he sat cradling her in his arms, he felt protective and proud that he'd been able to calm her. Her relaxed body and steady breathing indicated that she was asleep, so he gently lowered her body to the bed and was withdrawing from her embrace when she stirred.

"Don't go," she whispered, grasping his hand.

"Shhh. I'm not." There was a chair under the window and he pulled it close to the bed with his foot. He sank down onto the chair and rested his head against the wooden back. Her tiny hand had gone slack in his, and he knew she was slumbering again. Poor thing. How awful her life must have been for it to bring about such nightmares. He wanted to protect her, prove to her that she was safe with him.

The night was only half gone and he knew the remainder of it would be uncomfortable if he spent it in a hard chair. Nevertheless, he'd told her he would stay, and he was determined to keep his word.

fourteen

The morning light beckoned Sara, and she stirred under the cozy quilt. Even before she opened her eyes she had a vague notion that something had happened during the night. She stretched and opened her eyes. *What was that chair doing there?* Memories came flooding back in a torrent of humiliation. She'd had another nightmare. And this time there had been an audience.

She covered her face with her hands. What must he think of her? Thrashing around in her bed, then clinging to him like paint to a barn. And asking him to stay! She buried her face in the pillow and groaned. If only she could stay there the rest of the day.

Instead, she hauled herself from the bed and donned her oldest frock, since she knew she'd be working in the garden today.

After reviewing her Bible study of the previous evening, Sara said a quick prayer and joined Hetty in the kitchen.

The men had gotten an early start and had grabbed their own breakfast. At least she wouldn't have to face Nathan yet. Hetty and Sara fixed themselves a simple meal of oatmeal and toast. Sara was reflecting on her Bible study when Hetty interrupted her thoughts.

"You're awful quiet this mornin'."

"I guess I'm just deep in thought. I read something in the Bible that has me troubled."

"Anything you wanna talk about?"

"Actually, yes. I was hoping you might have some

answers for me. I was in the eighteenth chapter of Matthew, and I came across some verses about forgiveness."

Hetty refilled her coffee cup. "You mean the ones about forgiving 'Until seventy times seven'?"

"Yes, that's it. I guess I'm confused about whom that applies to. I know Jesus was saying, in effect, that we should forgive a person over and over, but He surely didn't mean that we should forgive everyone for everything. Aren't there sins that are unworthy of forgiveness? What about people who aren't even sorry for what they did? Do we have to forgive them?"

"You're talkin' about your stepfather."

"I guess I am," Sara said.

"There are other verses about forgiveness that you might want to look at. I'll jot a few of them down for you later, but I'm afraid you're not gonna like what they have to say. There are a couple of verses in Matthew, in the sixth chapter, that say, 'For if ye forgive men their trespasses, your heavenly Father will also forgive you: But if ye forgive not men their trespasses, neither will your Father forgive your trespasses.' "

"You mean, if I don't forgive Pete, God won't forgive me?" Sara asked in dismay.

"I'm afraid that's right, dear."

"But how can I forgive him, Hetty? After what he did to my mother and me, how can I just say it's okay? He wasn't sorry. Not even the next day, after he was sober." Her eyes filled with tears as the enormity of the task engulfed her.

Hetty reached over to lay a hand over hers. "I've never had to forgive someone for somethin' as cruel as what your stepfather did to you and your mama, but I can tell you this: Forgivin' doesn't mean condonin' what he did. It's not sayin' that his hittin' was okay. Forgiveness is releasin' him from responsibility—not holdin' him accountable anymore. Even that won't be easy. I'll be prayin' for you, that God will take away your anger and enable you to forgive him."

"I appreciate that, Hetty. You've given me a lot to think about."

"You know, it might be easier to forgive him if you look at the good that's come out of it."

"What do you mean?"

"You've heard the story of Joseph from the Bible?"

"You mean the boy who had a coat of many colors?"

"Yep, that's the right one, but there's a heap more to his story than that coat. His daddy gave it to him because Joseph was his favorite child. His eleven brothers became terrible jealous and ended up sellin' him as a slave to a bunch of strangers."

"His own brothers did that?"

"Yep, and that's not all. They told their father Joseph had been killed by a wild animal. Then, while Joseph was in Egypt, he was put in prison, through no fault of his own. I can't recall how long he was there, but it seems like it was years."

"Why, Hetty? Why did God let all those awful things happen to him?"

"I was just getting to that. Pharaoh had a dream that needed interpreting, and God gave the answer to Joseph. It ended up saving the Egyptian people from seven years of famine. Since Joseph had done that, Pharaoh put him in charge of all of Egypt."

"Oh. So Joseph was rewarded with a good life. Still, he must have hated his brothers after what they'd done to him."

"Actually, Joseph had a chance to confront his brothers during the famine. They came to Egypt hoping to get food for their families."

Sara smiled smugly. "I'll bet he sent them on their merry way!"

"Nope! To make a long story short, he told them he forgave them."

"Forgave them! But they'd sold him, for goodness sakes!"

"Yes, but Joseph's heart was right with God, and God saw to it that He worked things out for Joseph's own good. It even says that in the Bible after Joseph forgives his brothers. I can't quote it by heart, but it says somethin' like, 'You intended to harm me, but God turned it into somethin' good.'"

"So, you're saying that Pete intended to hurt me, but God made something good of it all?"

"Well, if your stepfather hadn't been violent, where would you be?"

"In Boston still, I suppose," Sara said.

"And you wouldn't be married to Nathan and livin' on this ranch. I, for one, would be sorry about that!"

"I never looked at it that way. I suppose God has brought good out of a bad situation."

"He has a way of doin' that." Hetty drained her coffee and stood. "We have a heap of work ahead of us today, and here it is 7:00 already!"

They cleaned the floor downstairs, which took most of the morning. Hetty's knee was acting up, so she stayed in the house to make bread and mend while Sara slipped on a pair of gloves and set to work weeding the garden. It was hot, dirty work, but she found it rewarding. Their seeds had sprouted, and as she worked she anticipated the vegetables they would enjoy.

When it was nearly time to fix supper, Hetty came out to the garden.

"How's it comin'?"

"Let's just say I hope I'm pulling weeds and not our vegetables!"

Hetty laughed. "I'm sure you're doin' fine."

"Look at me! I look as if I've been rolling in the dirt!" Sara said.

"That's why I came out a little early. I fixed you a bath in the kitchen. Thought you might like to get cleaned up before supper."

Sara sat back on her heels. "Oh, Hetty, you're a godsend!"

"Well, the best cure for a hot day like this is a dip in Willow Spring, but a bath will have to suffice for today."

Sara tugged off her gloves and started into the house with Hetty. "What's Willow Spring?"

"It's a lovely spot here on the ranch. It's a good ride, but well worth it. There's a stream that comes down from the hills and into a big pool of water. We call it Willow Spring because of all the weeping willow trees on the banks."

"I just realized how little I've seen of the ranch," Sara said.

"We'll have to fix that soon."

Sara went into her room and gathered some clean clothes, then walked to the kitchen. She shut the door for privacy, and enjoyed a short bath in the tepid water. After dressing, Hetty helped her dump the bathwater, then they started supper.

By the time Nathan and Gus arrived, supper was well under way. The men got comfortable and sipped a glass of iced tea while waiting for the meal.

The previous night's episode was a distant memory now, and time had eased the awkwardness between Nathan and Sara. The meal passed with casual conversation about the day's activities. When they were nearly finished, Hetty addressed Nathan.

"Sara was just telling me today how little she's seen of the ranch, Nathan. I thought maybe you'd like to show her around a little one day soon."

Nathan looked as if he'd been caught off guard for a moment, then cleared his throat. "I don't know why I didn't think of it myself. That's a great idea, Hetty. As a matter of fact, I don't have anything pressing tomorrow, as long as you don't mind carrying on without me, Gus."

"Not a bit. It's about time your wife saw more than the front yard of this ranch!"

Nathan turned to Sara. "How does that work for you?"

Sara's mouth had remained open through the entire discussion. "Oh. Well—it's just fine, I suppose. If you don't mind handling things around here, Hetty."

"Of course I don't. In fact, why don't we pack you a lunch, and you can have a picnic at Willow Spring." She addressed Nathan. "I was just tellin' Sara what a lovely spot it is."

"That's a fine idea," Nathan said. "We'll ride out after breakfast." He paused and looked at Sara. "You do ride?"

Sara hid a smile. "I think I can manage."

Hetty helped Sara pack a picnic after supper, since there would be little time for it in the morning. Gus hung around, too, and kept snatching food from the saddlebag. Hetty slapped his hand. "Gus, you get your hands outa that food!" She turned toward Sara. "That man's got an appetite that won't quit!"

"It's your cookin', woman! I just can't resist it!"

Sara smiled at their bantering, enjoying their special relationship. It was clear they adored one another. She hoped one day she and Nathan could share such a close rapport.

Once the bag was packed, Hetty and Gus went home.

The evening was spent in quiet companionship, Nathan reading his Bible, and Sara working on her needlepoint. When darkness closed in upon them, they turned in, each looking forward to a day of leisure.

As Sara lay in bed that night, she remembered Hetty's words about forgiveness.

God, I don't want anything to come between You and me. You know my heart. You know I have anger against Pete for what he did to Mama and me. I don't know how to forgive him. I've never had to do anything like this before, and I'm not even sure how to begin. So I guess I'm asking You for help. Pastor Hill says You are capable of anything, and I know now that You care. Maybe You could take these feelings away from me—help me not to be angry or bitter toward him anymore. Well, that's all I have to ask for now, God. Oh, and please bless my day with Nathan tomorrow. Amen.

&

By the time the sun peeked over the hills, Nathan had the horses saddled and ready to go.

It was already warm and, since the sky was unmarred by clouds, Sara knew the day would be a hot one. She had on her lilac dress, which was her coolest, and a bonnet to shield her face from the sun.

She left the house to join Nathan by the corrals where he waited with his stallion and an appaloosa.

"All set?" Nathan asked.

"Yes." She walked to the horse and stroked her face. "What's her name?"

"Jenny. There's no need to be nervous; Jenny's real agreeable. She won't do anything unless you tell her to. Only Thunder here can outrun her, but she won't go fast without a command."

Sara was glad Nathan was behind her and couldn't see her grin.

"I don't have a sidesaddle, so I'm afraid you'll have to ride astride."

"That's okay. This is a full skirt, so I can manage."

Sara positioned herself to mount, but before she could get a foot in the stirrup, Nathan stepped up behind her. "Here, let me help."

"That's okay, I can—" Before she could finish, he boosted her into the saddle as if she weighed nothing. He adjusted the stirrups, and she slipped her boots into them.

"Does that feel comfortable?"

"Perfect," she said.

He mounted his own horse, which was black and at least a hand taller than her own.

They set out for the western pasture, talking some as they went. After a few minutes, Nathan said, "You doing okay?"

"Just fine! How about a race?" she said, feeling renewed joy at being able to ride again.

Nathan laughed as if it were a joke.

"Say, from here to that cluster of dogwoods?" She barely gave Nathan a chance to recover from shock. "Ready, go!"

"Sara! I don't think. . ."

She shot off, and his words were swallowed by the wind as Jenny dug her hooves into the packed earth. A smile stretched across her mouth as she flew over the prairie. Oh, she had missed this! She bent down low to the horse's neck. Her bonnet slid off and thumped against her back in perfect rhythm with Jenny's gait.

Nathan was right: Jenny was a fast horse! Her head start had given her an advantage, but as she neared the copse of trees, she heard hooves rumbling by her side. Thunder had just passed Jenny when they reached the designated stopping point. Nathan and Sara reined in their mounts.

Sara looked at Nathan, breathless, her shining eyes revealing her excitement. He was looking at her with something akin to astonishment.

"You little sneak! You ride like a cowboy! Letting me think you were a greenhorn!"

Sara laughed delightfully. "I never told you that! You just assumed it!"

"Well, I sure was wide of the mark!" There was admiration in his eyes as they sat grinning at each other, before she turned away to hide her embarrassment.

Sara's pins had fallen from her hair during the ride, so she left it down and tied her bonnet in place. If Nathan truly liked her hair, it couldn't hurt to let him see it.

They resumed their ride, keeping the horses' pace at a walk to let them catch their breath. Nathan talked about the ranch and its history. She was fascinated to learn about the place she'd be spending the rest of her life. He told her about the blizzard of '86 and how costly it was to the ranchers of the area. They talked about the dry spring weather and its effect on the crops and cattle. There would be enough feed for Nathan's cattle because they had put up hay, but many of the ranchers would have to buy hay.

Along the way they saw various wildlife—deer, prairie chickens, rabbits. There were buffalo, too, he said, but many had been killed.

By the time the sun was high in the sky, Sara was eager to have her feet on the ground. It had been years since she'd ridden for so long, and she dreaded the soreness she knew she'd feel in the morning.

Soon, she heard the trickling of water and was relieved to hear Nathan say they'd reached Willow Spring. They dismounted and led their horses under the willow branches to the water's edge.

"Oh! This is lovely! What a beautiful spot!" The spring was large and clear. The edges were grassy, and there was a shelf of rock along part of the bank. She stood on the outcropping and let Jenny drink her fill.

"This is the best site on the ranch, I think," Nathan said.

When the horses were finished, Nathan tethered them to a tree and removed the saddlebag and blanket.

"Here, I'll do that," Sara said.

Nathan surrendered the pouch and knelt on the bank to wash his hands and face while Sara spread the blanket under a tall willow. It was comfortable in the shade, and since there was no threat from the sun, she removed her bonnet.

She offered Nathan a glass of lemonade, then poured one for herself. "I'm so thirsty; I think I could drink the whole spring!"

"It is hot today."

She spread the food out on the blanket, and Nathan took a seat across from her. After saying grace, Nathan tore off a chunk of bread and handed it to Sara. "So tell me, where'd you learn to ride like that?"

Sara smiled. "My father used to train horses for a wealthy family outside of Boston. I grew up there on the horse farm. The owner allowed us to ride whenever we pleased. My father was quite a horseman, and he taught me to ride when I was very young. I don't remember *not* knowing how to ride."

"You've never mentioned your father."

"He died when I was fourteen. My mother and I rented a little house in Boston. We had to sell one of our horses to afford it. Mama sewed to bring in a little extra money when I was still in school. Money ran out when I was fifteen, and she married Pete. He sold our only other horse, and I haven't ridden since."

"Well, I can tell you haven't forgotten anything!"

"I've been longing to ride one of your horses since I arrived here. It felt wonderful to be in a saddle again!"

"You only had to ask. You're welcome to ride anytime."

"Thank you."

They ate in silence for a moment while Nathan gazed at the water as if he were deep in thought. "Me and my dad used to ride out here and frolic in the water when I was a boy. He taught me how to swim here."

"How deep is it?"

"It's only waist deep in the middle." He winked at her. "That's neck deep to you." She tossed a towel at him, and he laughed.

When they finished eating, Nathan pulled off his boots and socks. "I don't know about you, but I'm going to take advantage of that cool water."

"I'll join you in a minute." Sara packed up the leftovers, leaving the blanket on the ground. She removed her boots and peeled off her stockings.

The grass prickled her sensitive feet as she tiptoed to the rock ledge. Most of the water was shaded, but there were specks of brilliance where the sunlight filtered through the trees.

Sara gathered her skirt in one hand and dipped in a toe. "That feels heavenly!"

Nathan was up to his knees in the pool, heedless of his trousers. "Watch yourself when you get in. The water's about a foot deep off that ledge."

Sara stepped in, raising her skirt high enough to keep it dry. A flush rose to her cheeks when she saw Nathan watching. Her legs had been exposed clear to her knees!

She was so busy reminding herself that Nathan *was* her husband, that she didn't even notice the temperature change when she entered the water.

"Is it too cool for you?"

"What? Oh—no, it feels just wonderful!"

They walked around the spring, along the edges, where it was shallower. Nathan paused here and there to point out a small creature.

"The town is named for a larger spring on the other side of town. You can guess what's growing on the banks."

"Cedar trees?" she said, smiling.

"Right. It's bigger, but nowhere near as pretty, in my unbiased opinion."

"Unbiased, huh?" She teased him with her eyes.

His lips twitched. "One day I'll take you there and let you judge for yourself."

As they neared the rock outcropping once again, an impish idea formed in Sara's mind. She bent over and looked into the sparkling liquid. "Look, Nathan! What's that?" She had her finger in the water, pointing at something, but it was hard to see past the sun-dappled surface.

"What?" he said.

"That thing. . .right there."

Nathan bent down, trying to peer into the changing water. "I don't see anything." He bent lower. "What does it. . .?"

In one motion Sara opened her hand in the water and brought it up quickly, splashing Nathan.

She giggled as he straightened abruptly, rivulets of water streaming down his face. For a moment he looked stunned, but that expression was swiftly replaced by another look.

Sara covered her grin with a hand and began to slowly retreat. "Now, Nathan, it was just a little water, and I was only teas—"

Nathan sprang forward, and Sara squealed as she turned to scamper up the rock ledge. She ran over the grass and around a tree, unaware of the rough ground. Before she could round the tree, Nathan's arm caught her around her waist. "Oh, no, you don't."

He lifted her into his arms. Sara tried futilely to escape as he walked with purpose to the bank and into the water.

"Nathan, what are you. . . ?" When he halted, she suddenly realized what he had in mind. "You can't throw me in there! I'll get all wet!"

"Uh-huh!"

He swung her body away from the water for momentum, and she shrieked as his arms carried her back over the water. She braced herself for the cold plunge, but rather than releasing her, he swung her body back to his.

She opened her eyes. "You beast! You nearly scared me to death!" she scolded.

His eyes twinkled. "A beast, am I? Why, I think a beast would give you a good soaking. Yes, I think so." He made to toss her out again, but she clutched his neck and implored.

"Please! You're not a beast! You're—you're a—a fine gentleman, that's what you are! Yes. And a gentleman would never throw a lady into cold water!"

He paused as if contemplating the word. "Hmm. . .gentleman. I think I like the sound of that. Maybe I'll let you off the hook this time." He waded to the ledge and released her legs. Her body slid down his until her feet found the rocky surface. The tall sill added to her height, and when she looked into his playful eyes, she found they were nearly even with hers.

Her arms slid to his shoulders, but his hands remained at her waist. As she gazed at him, all teasing fell away, and his expression grew serious. There was heat in his ashen eyes, and she felt herself drawn to them, mesmerized. Everything around them faded away until there was nothing else but those eyes.

Her gaze dropped to his lips of their own accord, and she watched them move as he spoke. "If you keep looking at me like that, I'm going to kiss you."

She raised her eyes to his, then deliberately glanced at his mouth again.

He lowered his head and tested her mouth with his warm lips. Sara felt almost dizzy as she responded. Never had she felt anything like this. Their wedding kiss had been pleasant, but the power of this kiss left her feeling weak and in awe.

He stepped away too soon, and she knew her eyes mirrored her thoughts.

"We'd best get started if you want to see the rest of the ranch," he said softly.

She blinked and made a valiant effort to pull herself together. "Yes, you're right," she said with more conviction than she felt.

They put on their boots in silence, each entertaining their own private thoughts. Sara was berating herself for responding without any restraint whatsoever. Nathan probably thought she was utterly wanton, she guessed. Why, she'd practically begged him to kiss her! Her face colored at the thought.

Across from her, Nathan was watching the delightful blush climb her cheeks, and wondered at its cause. Sara's mind would have been put to rest if she'd known Nathan's thoughts at that moment. He had thoroughly enjoyed the embrace and had decided he would let God lead in their relationship.

No more guarding his heart. He would allow this seed to

grow and see what happened. If it was anywhere near as good as he now suspected it could be, it would be worth risking his heart.

Not that he was comfortable with this new role. What did he know about being a husband? After all, he'd never even seen his mother and father together. There were some things that just came natural; as for the rest, he was in new and untried waters. He knew he wanted to touch Sara more, had held himself back in the past. There had been many a night that she'd sat stroking that dog's fur and he'd been jealous. Jealous—of a dog!

She was his *wife*. From now on, he'd touch her if he was so inclined. He felt a smile tug at the corner of his lips. She'd certainly seemed willing to have his touch a minute ago.

Sakes alive! He'd never experienced a kiss like that one. How could such a tiny woman make him feel all coiled up inside?

⁓

Tension eased between the two as the afternoon progressed. They talked about the ranch and other neutral topics until they were on comfortable ground once again. They even raced again, but Sara had no head start this time, and Nathan won by two lengths. She was impressed by his stallion and told him so.

Later, the conversation turned to the lunch-box social scheduled to take place on the coming Saturday. Sara had never been to one, but it was an annual tradition in Cedar Springs.

Nathan explained how it worked. All the ladies, married and single, would prepare a lunch in a basket. One at a time they would be auctioned off to the highest bidder, and proceeds were donated to the school. He said many of the wives marked their baskets by a ribbon so their husbands would be sure to bid on their lunches, and that there was much revelry during the social—but it was all in good fun. Sara was considering her own lunch basket, and when she gathered the courage, she spoke. "Would you like me to tie a ribbon on my basket?"

Nathan smiled wide, and Sara thought he looked pleased with the idea. "I'd like that very much," he said. "How about the blue one you wore on the day you arrived?"

Sara stared at him, speechless that he remembered. "All right. The blue one it is."

The rest of the afternoon passed quickly, but Sara was glad to see the house come into view. She was stiff, and her backside ached badly.

During dinner, Hetty wanted to know all about their explorations. Sara told her that Willow Spring was everything she'd said it was. They talked about the time they spent there, and Hetty's sharp eyes didn't miss the look that passed between the couple.

After dinner was cleared, Sara read her Bible while Nathan did some paperwork at the table.

Sara was just considering turning in when Nathan gathered his papers and stood. "I think I'll head on up to bed now." He ambled over to the small desk near Sara and set his papers down. Without warning, he dropped a kiss on her forehead. "Good night."

Sara wasn't sure if she replied or not. She just sat, her Bible resting in her lap, watching Nathan until he disappeared up the stairs.

fifteen

The next morning, Sara's body was as stiff and sore as she'd expected. Getting out of bed and into her clothes was such a chore, she wondered how she'd manage the rest of the day. However, the stiffness eased as she moved about, and she was able to forget her soreness for a while.

The next two mornings were not much better, and Sara determined that she would start riding again soon to accustom her body to the activity. On the second day, Hetty made an ointment for her, which she applied in the morning and evening. It was some help.

Nathan clearly felt guilty over Sara's incapacitation. She tried her best not to hobble in his presence, but it was especially difficult in the morning and evening hours. Each night she waited for him to retire first so that he wouldn't have to see her limp off to bed; her body stiffened up after sitting a while. Every night he pressed a kiss upon her brow.

By Saturday morning she felt much better, and after applying the liniment, her legs were good as new.

After breakfast, Sara and Hetty prepared their lunches for the lunch-box social. They fixed fried chicken together, and each added other food to make their meals unique.

Nathan and Gus had ridden over to Luke's house to lend him a hand, and Sara and Hetty were to take the carriage to town and meet the men there.

When Sara finished her basket, she proudly tied her ribbon to it. Hetty informed Sara that she had used the same basket for years, and Gus didn't need a ribbon to identify it. Having finished, they settled in the carriage and set off for town.

The bidding was to start at 11:00. Hetty said there were always at least a hundred people there, and some wouldn't get their lunch until well after 12:00.

It was a blustery day, but the warm sun made the temperature perfect. Fluffy clouds passed quickly, driven by the vigorous wind.

Sara wore her apricot gown and a matching bonnet. She had taken pains with her appearance today, and felt almost pretty. Hetty looked especially nice, too, and Sara told her so.

When they rode into town, Sara saw the crowd gathered on the church property. Families had spread quilts beneath trees, claiming prime spots in the shady grass. Some people sat around their blankets; others stood in small groups, chatting and laughing.

Sara and Hetty carried their baskets over to the tables that had been set up beside the church. As they approached the tables, Sara was dismayed to see that Mara was one of the two women tending the table. The other woman was serving lemonade, leaving Mara to take the baskets.

"Hello, Hetty. Sara." Her voice was sugary, but her smile resembled a sneer.

They returned the greeting, but wandered off after they left their baskets and obtained their drinks.

Sara and Hetty joined Laura and her mother under a large oak, on the other side of the church. If Sara had turned around, she would have seen Mara walking hurriedly to the general store and returning with a ribbon strikingly similar to the one on Sara's basket. She also would have seen Mara's haughty expression as she secured the ribbon to her own basket.

After a while, Nathan and Gus joined their wives around Laura's blanket. Sara learned that Laura's father had a job that required him to travel a great deal. Sara had assumed he was no longer living since Mrs. Reed was always alone. However, he was home this weekend, and Mrs. Reed pointed him out.

Shortly before 11:00 Nathan excused himself to get a cup of lemonade. Sara watched covertly as he approached the refreshment table. Mara hurried over to serve him, and Sara's heart sank as she saw Nathan smile and greet her. He didn't stay long, but seeing them together was enough to put a damper on her spirits.

Nathan joined Luke and Caleb, Luke's younger brother, just as the bidding began. Elizabeth, Luke and Caleb's eleven-year-old sister, was playing with several other young girls.

The porch of the small church was being used as a stage, and Reverend Hill was officiating as auctioneer. He opened with a prayer, then received the first basket from Mara's hands. It turned out to be Mrs. Reed's basket, and it was dutifully purchased by Mr. Reed for the tidy sum of forty cents. Sara and Hetty moved closer to the stage in order to give the Reeds some privacy, while the couple met at the platform to collect the basket.

Several other lunches were auctioned off to people whom Sara didn't know. There was laughing and teasing from the crowd, especially when there were two bidders competing for the same lunch.

Hetty's lunch was next, and Gus vied with Caleb for a good five minutes before Caleb forfeited. There was much laughter as Gus nailed Caleb with an exaggerated scowl for driving the bid up to one dollar.

Shortly after that, Laura's lunch was up for bidding. She blushed as several young men contended for the privilege of her company. They were all persistent, but Daniel Parnell was the one who sauntered away with Laura on his arm.

Sara stood alone now, wishing her lunch would be auctioned soon. Even as she thought this, the reverend held up a basket with a blue ribbon. She saw that it wasn't her basket, but the ribbon looked like hers.

Nathan began the bidding, and several others joined in, assuming that it was Sara's basket. There was no way to gain Nathan's attention, though, for he was surrounded by a throng. She was torn between amusement that he was bidding so tenaciously for the wrong basket, and disappointment that he wasn't going to be her lunch partner. It was evident by his resolve that he would come out on top, so Sara wasn't surprised when his bid was the highest at a dollar and thirty cents.

The crowd's applause turned to laughter when Mara Lawton came forward to claim her basket.

sixteen

Sara was so deep in thought that she didn't see Nathan's look of shock and dismay when he saw the owner of the basket. It was quickly replaced with a resigned grin.

Several people turned to smile good-naturedly at Sara, and she pinned a smile to her face. But inside she agonized.

Had this been a simple mistake, or had Nathan known it was Mara's lunch? They had spoken briefly before the bidding began. Perhaps she had shown him which basket was hers.

Reverend Hill continued to auction off baskets while Sara stood motionless, mortified that Nathan had chosen another woman's lunch. Never mind that the crowd thought it was a mistake. *She* knew.

To make matters worse, her basket was one of the last to be auctioned and there were few bidders left. Luke was the only one to bid on her lunch. It cost him thirty cents. She collected her basket in a daze and was grateful when he led her far away from Nathan and Mara. They settled on a large quilt, in the shade of an elm tree.

"Are you all right, Sara?" Luke asked

"I'm fine!" Her response was overbright, and Luke was perceptive enough to know she was bothered by Mara and Nathan lunching together. Since she clearly didn't want to discuss it, he set to work cheering her up. Luke was a story-teller; he had a gift for making others laugh.

A cat strolled by their blanket, curling around Sara's legs and purring a tune.

"We used to have a cat named Amos. He was a little thing, and we were devoted to him, but it was our pa he favored. Funny enough, Pa didn't like cats much, and the more he ignored Amos, the more that cat clung to him. And I do mean clung." He chuckled, and Sara waited for him to continue.

"Amos had a quirk that amused us: He didn't like to be left alone. Somehow he must have figured out that when we all dressed up in our finest clothes, we'd leave him to go to church.

"One Sunday we all hopped in the wagon—me, Caleb, and Beth in the back and Ma in the front. When Pa climbed in, we all saw something that nearly put us to tears." He smiled a wide, infectious grin. "Amos had somehow jumped onto Pa's back, and there he hung on his suit coat, clinging for dear life!"

They laughed together and Luke went on.

"Ma turned around and gestured for us not to say anything. All the way to church we talked and kept using expressions like 'let the cat out of the bag' and 'cat got your tongue'! We finally just lost it, and Pa figured out what was going on when Ma pointed to his back." He shook his head, still laughing. "Amos had to stay in the wagon during church, but he must've liked it, because every Sunday after that, he tried the same thing! Never did see such a cat!"

"I had no idea cats were so clever," she said as she stroked the tiger-striped feline. "My dog Blackie is the sweetest thing, but he's nowhere near that clever."

And so their conversation was steered toward animals. Sara was glad they weren't going to talk about Luke's parents, because she didn't want to make him sad. Hetty had told her that his folks had died two years earlier, leaving Luke, Caleb, and Elizabeth to run the ranch on their own.

Sara was developing a headache, but she enjoyed Luke's

company while they ate. He praised her cooking and made her laugh over and over. The meal passed surprisingly quickly, and when Sara consulted her timepiece, she was surprised to see that it was after 1:00. Luke helped her gather the plates and utensils and thanked her for the meal. They parted ways, and Sara looked about for Hetty. Her head was throbbing, and she hoped Hetty was ready to go home. When she spotted her under a shade tree with Gus, she made her way over to them.

"Having a good time, Sara?" Gus asked.

"It was a lovely time, but to be perfectly honest, I've developed a wretched headache, and I was wondering if you would mind if we left now, Hetty."

"Not at all, dear. In fact, I was just waitin' for you and Luke to finish up."

Gus carried the baskets to the wagon for them. As they walked, Sara was relieved to see Nathan talking to Mrs. Reed. At least he wasn't with Mara anymore.

Hetty must have noticed how quiet Sara was on the way home, for she began to talk to her about it. "Are you okay?"

"I'll be fine, I'm sure. I just need to lie down a while."

Hetty pressed on. "It sure is a shame you didn't get to share your lunch with Nathan. I know you worked real hard on it."

"Yes, well. . .Luke was good company and very appreciative of the food. Besides, I'm sure Nathan ate well, also." This last part was said with ill-disguised sarcasm.

Hetty, who was nothing if not perceptive, picked up on it.

"It was an accident, you know. At least on Nathan's part. Now Mara, on the other hand. . .well, I wouldn't put it past her to do somethin' so underhanded. She never made her feelings for Nathan a secret."

Sara was skeptical of Hetty's explanation. Her heart was in the right place, but she didn't have all the facts. She let the matter drop and watched the scenery go by. The clouds had multiplied since morning, and the temperature felt a bit cool now that the sun was veiled. The trees were waving in rhythm to the beat of the wind.

Sara drew in a breath and let out a sigh. She was deeply troubled over this thing going on between Nathan and Mara, and she didn't understand how Nathan could carry on in such a manner. He was a Christian, after all. There was a lot she didn't know about the Bible, but she did know that a man ought not give affection to a woman other than his wife.

She couldn't figure him out. He had been so kind to her lately, and the kiss at Willow Spring had been wonderful beyond words. At least for her.

A thought burst into her mind, causing an ache in her gut. What if she had been the only one enjoying that kiss? After all, he was the one who had ended it. And there hadn't been a second kiss. Perhaps he was only trying to make the best of their situation, and she was making too much of it. These thoughts discouraged her. She didn't want to fall in love with her husband if he was not going to love her in return! How awful to spend the rest of your life married to a man who didn't love you! *Oh, please, God—don't let that happen to me!*

Once they were home, Sara lay down and napped for a short time. When she awoke, she noted that her headache had dulled and the house was quiet. She went downstairs and found she was alone. The afternoon was spent in rare leisure, reading and quilting.

Hetty came in when it was time to get supper ready. They began eating when the men weren't home by a quarter past six, and they were still eating when Nathan and Gus came in. The ladies served up the plates, but it was Hetty who carried the conversation throughout the meal.

Sara knew she shouldn't be so withdrawn, but she was still smarting from the social that afternoon. No, it was more than that. She was hurting from this whole business between Nathan and Mara. Whether or not Nathan's bid on Mara's lunch was an accident didn't really matter.

She understood that Nathan would have married Mara if that were possible. But it didn't work out, so in order to save his ranch, he'd married Sara. She could accept that if it had ended there. But it hadn't. He'd married Sara—committed himself to her in the eyes of God—and now he was being unfaithful to her. He shouldn't have married her at all if he was unwilling to keep his vows.

Sara excused herself from the table and began washing the dishes while the others finished. She didn't see the look of concern that passed among the three at the table.

Hetty and Gus left shortly after, and Nathan settled himself in the main room with a book. The last thing Sara wanted was to be alone with him, so she decided to have a bath. She started the water heating on the stove and collected her nightgown. The kitchen door shut, she stripped off her clothes and sank into the large tin tub. She soaked for an hour, washing her hair and stalling, and when her skin was wrinkled and drawn, she emerged from the water. She hoped Nathan would be in bed. However, when she left the kitchen, she saw that was not the case.

Her long hair hung down her back in damp curls—wetting the thin white gown—as she padded barefoot to the stairs. She hoped she could go to bed without being noticed. She made it to the second step.

"Sara?"

She stopped on the step, but didn't turn around. "Yes, what is it?"

"I'd like to explain about this afternoon. . ."

"There's really nothing to talk about."

"You've been so quiet tonight. I'm sorry I didn't get to share your lunch. I want you to understand—"

"I understand perfectly, Nathan!" she shot out. "Good night."

She ascended the stairs quickly, leaving Nathan to stare after her with a familiar crease between his brows.

seventeen

The next week passed quickly. Hetty and Sara invited Luke, Caleb, and Elizabeth to supper one night. The brothers were entertaining company, to say the least.

Luke was a storyteller, whereas Caleb was the charmer. His looks were boyish compared to his older brother's, but he had a way of making people feel special. Sara imagined the young ladies were drawn to his chivalrous manner.

Little Elizabeth was a chatterbox. Her brown hair was plaited down both sides of her face, and her skin was browned from playing outdoors. Esther, the lady who watched Elizabeth and took care of the house, was given a rare evening off.

They had such a good time that Sara and Hetty promised to have them over again soon.

Nathan and Sara had fallen into their old pattern of avoiding one another. Sara was hurt over his betrayal, and she asked God every night to help her deal with her feelings. She didn't care to spend time with him and risk coming to care for him more. Therefore, each evening they went their separate ways.

If Hetty noticed the dissension between the two, she didn't say anything about it. The tension wasn't obvious when they were all together, at any rate. When Sara and Nathan were alone, however, strained silence loomed around them. Sara busied herself with a book or sewing in the evening, and Nathan usually read. He did try on several occasions to restore the harmony between them, and

Sara recognized those attempts for what they were.

By the end of the week she wondered if her detachment was a good idea. Nathan had begun to sit on the porch in the evenings, and Sara knew she was only driving him away—probably straight into Mara's arms.

She was pondering this possibility the next day as she rode Jenny through the pastures of bluestem grass. It was her first ride since she and Nathan had gone to the spring, and the fresh air was clearing her mind. She longed for the companionship she had shared with her husband such a short time ago.

She prayed as she rode back to the house that God would mend the rift between them and cause Nathan to end his relationship with Mara. She also thanked Him for the freedom she had from her stepfather.

Sara would remember with startling clarity the swiftness with which God answered the first part of that prayer.

The next day she and Hetty worked in the garden. Sara knelt down to extract a particularly stubborn weed. The ground was dry, and the dust had settled in her throat, hair, and clothes.

The garden required almost constant care, but the fruits of this labor were becoming evident with each new lime-colored plant that pushed its way through the warm soil. Soon there would be potatoes, peas, onions, and many other delicious vegetables. Sara's mouth watered at the thought, dampening her parched mouth. She needed a nice cool drink.

She had just pulled herself up to a standing position when the pounding of horse's hooves drew her attention. The rider was coming in at a fast pace. Out of the corner of her eye she saw Hetty rise to her feet and shield her eyes from the sun.

As the rider drew nearer, Sara identified him as Gus; but to her horror, she also saw a body draped across his lap.

"Dear Lord," she whispered, running to meet Gus at the front of the house. Her heart bottomed out as anxiety kicked in. She uttered an unintelligible prayer and knew dread when she recognized the heap on Gus's lap.

"What happened?"

Gus pulled back the reins and was dismounting before the horse halted. "He got gored by a bull. Open the door!"

Sara rushed to comply as Hetty rounded the corner. "Is he all right?"

"I don't know." Gus staggered up the stairs under the weight of his load.

Hetty gathered towels and set some water to boil while Sara followed Gus. He laid Nathan on top of the quilt, and Sara saw for the first time the extent of Nathan's injury. His shirt was saturated with blood and ripped where the bull's horn had torn into his flesh. She stood trembling while Gus placed his fingers on Nathan's neck to check for a pulse.

"He's alive. Pulse is faint. I'm goin' after Doc Hathaway." He rushed past a rigid Sara and stopped in the doorway. "It doesn't look good, Sara," he said gently before clamoring down the stairs and out the door.

Sara rushed to her husband's side and removed the shirt. Blood was flowing from the wound. Helplessness and despair closed in upon her like fog smothering a deep valley.

"Hetty!"

She heard footsteps bustling up the steps, and then Hetty hurried into the room with an armload of towels.

"I don't know what to do! He's bleeding, and I don't know what to do!"

Hetty put a towel over the wound and pressed against it with steady pressure. "Here, keep pushin' to stanch the blood flow." She left the room, and Sara pressed on the towels with most of her weight.

Please, God, don't take him from me. He doesn't even know how I feel! Please!

Sara didn't know how long she pressed on the wound. When the blood soaked through, she added another towel and kept pressing. Hetty came in with a jar of liquid, and a pot of boiled water, then scurried away after checking the wound. She soon returned with nearly every lamp in the house and had just finished lighting them when Gus came in, followed by Doc Hathaway.

After seeing that the bleeding had almost stopped, he asked the others to leave the room while he examined Nathan. Leaving her husband at that moment was one of the hardest things Sara had ever had to do.

Hetty grasped her arm. "Come on, dear. You've done everything you can do. Let Doc do his job." She guided Sara into the hallway. Gus shut the door behind him, and upon seeing Sara's tear-streaked face, he withdrew his handkerchief and offered it to her. She just stared at it, her mind too muddled to understand. Hetty took it and mopped the tears Sara had been unaware of.

They huddled together on the top stair, where they prayed and talked but mostly sat in silence, waiting for a word of hope. The doctor seemed to be taking forever.

At last the door opened, and the doctor emerged with a grim face. They all rose to their feet and looked at him with such desperation that he appeared to find his next words difficult to say.

"I'm afraid things don't look very good. He lost a lot of blood. Fortunately, the lungs weren't punctured. I fixed him up the best I could. But as I said, he lost a great deal of blood. The next twenty-four hours are critical. Try to force him to drink if he wakes. He needs to replace the blood he lost. The sooner he regains consciousness, the better."

"Isn't there more we can do?" Sara's glassy eyes pleaded.

"Pray. Pray that he hasn't lost too much blood, and then pray that infection doesn't set in."

"May I sit with him?"

"By all means. In fact, someone should be with him round-the-clock. If he awakens, give him liquids—broth and such."

"Thank you, Doctor," she whispered before entering Nathan's room.

Nathan lay unnaturally still on the bed. The doctor had put a blanket over him, and it was tucked under his chin. The harsh lighting made his features appear pasty white. It reminded her of her mother's appearance when she lay dead in her coffin. She pushed the thought from her mind and concentrated on the shallow rise and fall of his chest that reassured her of the life in his body.

She walked to his side and touched his face with hands that trembled. His skin was warm to the touch, and for the first time she allowed herself to caress the face she'd come to love.

"Nathan, you have to fight," she whispered. "Don't leave me now. Not when I've just realized. . ." She broke off as a sob burst forth.

Please, God, help him! Give him the strength to come through. And if You should desire to take him home with You, help me to bear the pain!

Sara pulled a chair up to the large bed, not wanting to jostle him, and sat holding his hand for a long time. Hetty brought lunch in to her, but she couldn't eat. She just talked to him, hoping he would somehow hear her and open his eyes, but her hope began to wane as the sun set and darkness fell. She had turned down all the lamps but one, and it seemed to cast an eerie glow on the room.

Hetty came in quietly and touched her shoulder. "Why don't you go lie down for a while, Sara? I'll sit with him."

"Thanks, Hetty, but I don't want to leave him." She looked at her with pain-filled eyes. "I have to be here in case he wakes up."

Hetty nodded. "I understand. I'm gonna sleep on the settee. I'll be downstairs if ya need anything."

"Thanks."

Sara dozed off and on that night, her hand resting on Nathan's. At one point she thought she felt him move and she bolted upright, studying his features. When nothing happened after several minutes, she leaned back and drifted off again, thinking she must have imagined it.

Hours later, the patter of rain against the windowpane roused Sara from a deep sleep. Her head was cocked to the side at an awkward angle, and she grimaced as she straightened her body.

Morning light flooded through the window, enabling her to see that Nathan's face had regained some color. She let her hand stroke his jawline, and the prickle of whiskers teased her fingers.

"Nathan?" she said.

Disappointment settled inside her at his lack of response. She had hoped a full night's rest would restore his body.

A clap of thunder sounded, and Sara praised God for the rain they'd all been praying for. She knew if circumstances had been different, the sound of rain would have sent the four friends laughing and dancing. As it was, the event no longer held such importance.

There was a quiet knock at the door, then Hetty entered with a tray of food.

"Any change?" Hetty asked.

"He hasn't awakened, but I think his color is better."

"Yes, it is. That's good." She laid the tray on the desk. "I know you prob'ly don't feel like eatin', but you need to keep up your strength if you're gonna be tendin' to Nathan."

"I am hungry, thanks."

Hetty handed her some bandaging supplies. "Doc left these. He said to change the bandages in the mornin' and evenin'."

"I will."

Gus stuck his head in the door. "How's he doin'?"

"His color's better, but no change other than that," Hetty said.

"You holdin' up, Sara?"

"I'm fine. Your wife's taking good care of me."

"Good. I've got chores waitin'. . .better get to 'em."

Hetty left shortly after Gus. Sara's rumbling stomach sent her to the plate of pancakes Hetty had brought. It had been twenty-four hours since her last meal, so she made quick work of the food. After eating, she went about changing Nathan's bandage. The doctor had cleaned the wound well, and Sara could see the line of tiny stitches that closed the skin. There was dried blood in the area surrounding the injury, so Sara used water from the pitcher to clean him gently. This was the first time she'd seen her husband without his shirt, and she admired his well-muscled chest as she worked.

She'd just rinsed the washcloth when she heard a low moan. Her head snapped around, and she watched as his eyelids fluttered.

"Nathan? Nathan!" Flinging aside the washcloth, she rushed to his side. "Nathan, open your eyes!" His eyelids fluttered again, encouraging her to continue her efforts. She put her hands on his face. "Nathan, it's Sara. Open your eyes and look at me!" He groaned again and turned toward her. "That's it! Come on, look at me." His eyes opened the tiniest bit and closed again. "Nathan McClain, now you listen to me! I want you to open your eyes this instant!"

It seemed to take supreme effort, but seconds later, tired gray eyes were staring into hers.

"That's it, Nate. How are you feeling?"

He wet his lips and closed his eyes for an instant. "Thirsty," he said with a scratchy voice.

"Oh! Here, let me get you some water." She poured a glass and took it to him. She tried to help him lift his head, but the strain on his stomach caused him to moan. Hetty must have heard the commotion, for she rushed in.

"Hetty, can you help me prop him up?"

Between the two of them, they were able to get two pillows under his head. Sara gave him the water and addressed Hetty. "Do you have that broth ready? The doctor said that would be best."

Hetty hurried to get it, but Nathan had no sooner rested his head on the pillows again than he fell sound asleep.

eighteen

Sara was eating lunch when Nathan awoke again. She shoved her tray aside and went to him. "Hello there. Do you want some water?"

He nodded, and she helped him drink. His eyes were on her when she returned with more water.

"What happened?" His voice was hoarse from lack of use.

"It was a bull. You don't remember?"

His eyes shut. "Yeah, I remember now." His eyes opened again. "When?"

"Yesterday morning."

"What time is it?"

"Noon. You've been asleep twenty-four hours. Are you in much pain?"

"I've had worse."

"I seriously doubt that."

Hetty brought the broth in then, and Sara fed it to him while Hetty checked his wound. As soon as Hetty took the bowl, Nathan dropped off to sleep.

۰

Nathan's condition improved over the next few days. He spent more time awake, and his appetite caught up with him.

At midweek, Doc Hathaway came to check on him and shook his head in wonder at Nathan's quick recovery. They all attributed it to the many prayers that had been lifted up for him. The doctor warned him that his body would require more time to heal, and admonished him to stay in bed for another week.

Nathan became a testy patient as he headed into his second week of confinement. Sara didn't take it personally, for she knew Nathan wasn't accustomed to being idle. His energy had returned and, except for the soreness in his middle, he felt like his old self. However, Sara was determined to follow the doctor's orders.

Even after all his complaining, she was not prepared to see him sitting on the settee when she came in from the garden. His breathing was labored, and his face was sallow. His mutinous gaze collided with hers.

"Nathan McClain! What in the world do you think you're doing, coming down those stairs by yourself? Why, to just think what could've happened—and me outside!"

She saw amusement flicker in his eyes. "You're beginning to sound like Hetty!" Sara flushed, and he continued. "Now, there's no sense in me lying in bed all day. I'm not up to ranching just yet, but there's no reason why I can't rest here on the settee. I'm as bored as a man can be up there!"

Sara considered his words, knowing he would find his own way downstairs if he wanted to. "All right. Just promise me you'll let someone help you up and down the stairs."

"It's a deal," he said, smiling.

She headed upstairs. "I'll just go get your pillows and book."

Nathan shook his head and muttered, "A regular mother hen."

≈

That night Sara lay in her bed with her eyes closed, but sleep would not come. She used the time to talk to God and, after a while, the Lord brought Pete to her mind. Sara's eyes snapped open when she realized that there was no anger in her heart. She deliberately thought of him again—thought of the awful way he treated her and her mother—and waited for the anger that usually rushed in.

It didn't come.

She lay staring at the ceiling in wonder. She didn't know when it had happened, but somewhere along the way, her anger had drained away. *I forgive him, Lord. Thank You for taking away my anger.* Sara's mouth turned up in a contented smile.

❧

Sara felt a new serenity. Her heart was at peace, and the rift between herself and Nathan was gone. Things were getting back to normal—except Nathan was confined to the house. She secretly delighted in his constant presence, although she knew it wouldn't last much longer; he was getting stir-crazy.

Friends and neighbors came calling to see for themselves that Nathan was on the mend. Many of the men offered to help Gus on the ranch, and he obligingly accepted. Laura and Mrs. Reed came by, as did Reverend Hill and his wife and, of course, Luke, Caleb, and Elizabeth. Visitors were to be expected at a time like this, and Sara greeted them at the door with a broad smile.

However, the welcome expression fled from her face one evening when Sara opened the door to find Mara standing there. She looked innocent-as-you-please in her fine clothing. She did not wear a hat, leaving her gold-spun hair to spill around her shoulders. Mara's chin tipped up, reminding Sara of her manners.

"Good evening, Mara. How may I help you?"

Her blue eyes widened. "Why, I'm here to see Nathan, of course."

Knowing Nathan was on the settee, Sara had no choice but to step aside and allow Mara to enter.

Upon seeing him, Mara gushed, "Oh, Nathan! I've been so worried about you! You poor dear. How wretched you must feel!"

Knowing it was the height of rudeness but not caring, Sara exited through the kitchen door without even offering tea. Mara had made it obvious that she felt Sara needed some lessons in etiquette anyway.

Sara walked in the woods beside the house. She was accompanied by Blackie, who ran ahead, then stopped and turned toward her abruptly, his tail waving in the air. He was in the mood to play, but Sara wasn't.

Things had been going so well. Nathan had resumed his nightly pecks on the forehead, and she was beginning to think he cared for her. She knew she cared for him—*loved* him. She had realized it while he was lying so close to death. Her heart ached at the thought of Nathan and Mara in the house alone.

She suddenly stiffened her back. That woman had no right to be in Sara's house alone with her husband!

She marched back to the house and was just about to yank open the side door when she heard the front door opening. She paused on the step, relieved to be avoiding Mara altogether. Her heart froze when she heard Mara's parting words.

"I'll see you next Friday evening then, Nathan. Good-bye until then."

Sara drew in a sharp breath. It couldn't be what it sounded like! It just couldn't! *But it is,* she thought as she sank down on the cool step. He was meeting her next Friday. Numbness flowed through her veins, mercifully filling the hole that had been gnawed within her.

She sat there until long after the carriage had clattered away. Darkness had descended upon the valley and Sara knew Nathan would want to go to bed soon. The tears had long since stopped flowing, but she wiped away any evidence of them with the hem of her gown and went inside.

There was a single lamp burning on the table beside Nathan. He turned toward her when the door clicked shut, and she saw that the light reflected off one side of his face, producing a warm glow. The shadows enhanced his angular jawline and, even from a distance, she could see the flickering of his eyes.

"I was beginning to worry," he said.

She moved into the room and stopped a good distance away from him. "I went for a walk."

His eyes narrowed as he studied her. "Is something wrong? If it's about Mara coming—"

"No. No, nothing's wrong. I just lost track of the time. Would you like some help upstairs?"

"Sure. Yeah. Think you could help me up?"

Sara walked to stand in front of him and took his hands when he held them out. This had been her method of helping him stand since the accident. She would lean back with all her weight and thus lever him up to standing.

Tonight, however, when she leaned back, Blackie passed behind her and she lost her footing. Nathan, who was nearly upright, pulled her toward him to keep her from falling backward. Their bodies came together with a thud, and Nathan brought his hands around her back to steady her.

The impact caused him to grunt, and she searched his face. "Are you all right?"

His smoky eyes fixed on hers, and she trembled under his heated gaze. "I'm fine," he whispered.

Sara watched in a daze as his head lowered. His eyes remained open as he brushed her lips with his own. Never had she experienced anything as moving as this.

His lips returned to hers, desperate, like a starving man at a potluck supper. She feasted with him, savoring every crumb, until doubts slowly began to creep in. He was kissing her, but was he loving Mara? Was he imagining she was Mara even now? Tears gathered behind her lids, and she choked back a sob as she pushed against his shoulders.

Her eyes were trained on his shirt, but she felt his reluctance to withdraw.

"Sara?" he said, tipping her chin up until he could read the misery in her eyes. "What's wrong? Did I hurt you?"

She shook her head, dislodging his hand. "No. I–I'm just tired, that's all. It's been a long day. . ." Making an effort to collect herself, she lifted her lips in a smile that didn't quite reach her eyes. "We'd best get you up to bed."

She helped him up the stairs in silence. When they reached the landing, she bade him good night and made a hasty retreat to her room.

৯

Nathan watched in confusion as she scuttled away. Something obviously was troubling her. He thought through the events of the evening and realized she'd been fine until Mara arrived. He'd been surprised that she left the house without offering tea or coffee, as she had with all the other callers. Not that he cared one way or the other if Mara was made to feel welcome. In his opinion, she'd overstayed her welcome, and he certainly hadn't wanted to be alone with the woman. He'd even been irritated when Sara left him to deal with her alone. The less he saw of Mara, the better.

Ever since that lunch-box social, he'd suspected that Sara was bothered by Mara. Tonight just confirmed it. Regardless of her denial, he was sure there had been some kind of misunderstanding.

He considered clearing it all up in the morning, but he

didn't want Sara making an issue of Friday night. Nathan had promised months ago to help Mr. Lawton install a new water closet in their house, and there was no honorable way out.

No, this would just have to wait. Friday was only six days away. He'd have to bide his time until then.

nineteen

For the first time in two weeks Nathan was able to attend Sunday services. Sara had a difficult time keeping her mind on the sermon, for Nathan was sitting very close, his leg pressed against hers.

She had awakened that morning feeling disheartened. It seemed there would be no end to this relationship between Mara and her husband. The woman wasn't in church today, but next Friday loomed in Sara's mind like a menacing cloud.

Out of nowhere, Sara heard Reverend Hill say the word "peace," and her attention snapped back to the sermon, for peace was exactly what she needed. He asked the congregation to turn to John 16:33. Sara followed along in her Bible as he read. "These things I have spoken unto you, that in me ye might have peace. In the world ye shall have tribulation: but be of good cheer; I have overcome the world."

Sara was still pondering these words when Reverend Hill turned to Romans 5:1–2. "Therefore being justified by faith, we have peace with God through our Lord Jesus Christ: By whom also we have access by faith into this grace wherein we stand, and rejoice in hope of the glory of God."

Sara made a conscious effort to memorize the locations of these verses. She wanted to commit them to memory and read the verses near them.

During the benediction she prayed that God would help her find peace in this marriage of hers. A peace that passes all understanding. Were those words in the Bible? They sounded very familiar. There was so much she didn't know.

The next day, Nathan began doing light work, with the doctor's approval. Sara and Hetty got back into their familiar routine. There was work to be caught up on: weeding, mending, groceries. Sara was grateful for the busy workload since it kept her from dwelling on her troubles.

Late that afternoon, as Mr. Parnell loaded some items into the back of the wagon, Mrs. Leighton from the post office came running toward her, waving an envelope.

"Mrs. McClain! I have a letter for you!"

Sara stepped away from the wagon and received the envelope. "Thank you, ma'am. You didn't have to trouble yourself." Sara peeked at the writing and recognized Helen's swirly script.

"Well, I didn't know how long it'd be before you stopped in. It's not every day you receive a letter, after all!"

"No, ma'am. And thank you."

After Mrs. Leighton went on her way and Mr. Parnell had finished, Sara climbed up into the wagon and tore the envelope open. Patience had never been one of her strong points, and Sara couldn't help but wonder why Helen was writing her when they'd agreed to cut off all ties for a while.

Sara unfolded the paper and began reading.

Dear Sara,

Oh, how I've missed you! It seems years since we've seen one another, and I for one am glad to break the silence!

I know if I write any more gibberish you are simply going to skip down to the part where I tell you what's going on, so I'll just put you out of your misery right now (wonderful friend that I am!).

I read in yesterday's paper that an unknown man

had stepped in front of a wagon and was killed. The description fit Pete's (they even said the man had been drunk), so of course I checked into matters. I'm sure you'll be relieved to know that the man was, in fact, your miserable stepfather, and you need not ever worry yourself about him again! Apparently he'd been coming from a saloon and just walked out into the street without a care. He was dragged for a ways before they could stop the horses. My only regret, dear friend, is that this didn't happen months ago! Now, here you are hundreds of miles away.

Sara sagged back on the bench. The news left her feeling numb—not at all how she would have thought she'd feel. There was even something more. Pity. Yes, she was certain it was pity she felt for this man who had no one to grieve his passing. What a wretched way to die. She continued to read.

Enough about me! How are you and your new husband getting along? I do hope that your life there is everything you deserve! Please write, as I am so very curious!

I went by your old house and left your landlord a note saying that I would remove your belongings. I'm sure there are things you miss and things of your mother's that you would like to have. I will have them sent to you as soon as you write and let me know you are still there (maybe a little longer, since I need my next paycheck for food and rent).

I'm looking forward to your letter, so be quick about it, please!

Your dearest friend,
Helen

Sara reread the end of Helen's letter and a smile formed on her face. She'd missed her friend's wit, and now they could write one another. And she would be able to get her belongings back! She had thought they were gone forever. She made a mental note to send Helen the money to ship them.

She carefully tucked the letter into her apron pocket and set off for home.

When she returned to the ranch, Hetty was on her knees in the garden, weeding. After unhitching the team, Sara left the parcels in the wagon and took her letter to Hetty.

"Did we get a letter?" Hetty sat back on her heels.

"I did. It's from my friend, Helen. I've mentioned her to you a time or two."

"That's wonderful! But I thought you two agreed not to write, given the circumstances."

Sara gave a rueful smile and handed Hetty the letter. "It seems the circumstances have changed."

Hetty removed her gloves and began reading. She was quiet and thoughtful as she read it, except for when she punctuated various parts with exclamations of surprise and dismay. When she finished she handed the paper back to Sara.

"She sounds like quite a gal, your friend."

"She is. I've missed her."

"You must have mixed feelins' about this news."

Sara stared off toward the hills. "You're right, I do. Mostly I feel, I don't know, indifferent. But I also feel a little sorry him. His life was so empty. He didn't know what it was to care about someone. Am I making any sense?"

"You're not only makin' sense, I'm right proud of you, Sara. Most folks would feel that he done got what he deserved. You're learnin' about God's ways mighty fast."

"Don't give me too much credit. I do feel a bit relieved that he's gone."

"Well, I reckon that's natural. 'Specially if you was worried he might find ya. Your friend'll be glad to hear your marriage has turned out good."

Hetty talked on for a while, but Sara's mind wandered on to her marriage problems. Things were not as good as Hetty thought they were. Sara needed to do some searching, both in the Bible and within herself.

≥a

Before bed that night, Sara studied the verses the reverend had read, as well as the chapters that contained them. The fifth chapter of Romans held special significance for Sara. It spoke of tribulations and how they give rise to patience. It also referred to the "free gift" Sara had received not so long ago. It was encouraging to have her faith reaffirmed through the Scriptures.

That week she and Hetty spoke often about those verses. Hetty was a seasoned Christian and had a wisdom that Sara prayed for. She didn't confide in Hetty about Nathan and Mara, for she didn't think it was her place to confess Nathan's indiscretions. She did, however, spend much time in prayer, asking God to guide her and help her endure the pain of betrayal.

Her anguish didn't vanish, but through God she found hope, and the capacity to forgive Nathan. She was even able to put herself in his place and realize the awful pain he must be suffering. To be in love and have to marry another. It was agonizing to think on this—that her husband felt a deep, abiding love for another. Sometimes it felt as if her heart would rend in two. The love she bore for her husband was not returned, for he had given his heart to someone else.

The ache was almost too much to bear at times. It was during these moments that she leaned upon the Lord, asking for strength to sustain her. She didn't allow herself to think about the difficult years that might lay ahead, but instead she merely took one day at a time.

She tried to maintain her relationship with Nathan that week, not wanting a wall to be erected between them again, but it was impossible to overlook the heavy gloom that had descended upon the house. She was sure Nathan felt it, too, although he didn't question her, and he continued his nightly pecks. He seemed in every way the loving husband, and if she hadn't known about Mara, she would consider herself the most blessed woman in the world.

Inevitably Friday arrived, and Sara woke with a sense of foreboding. She was uneasy all day. Chores were done and meals attended to, but underneath, Sara's stomach churned with apprehension. When Hetty asked about her distraction, Sara just asked her to pray for Nathan and left it at that.

It was 4:00 when Sara heard Nathan ride in from the west pasture. She was working in the garden, up to her elbows in dirt. Nathan disappeared into the stable and came out sometime later with their two bays, which he hitched to the wagon. When he was finished, he walked over to the garden.

Sara ran a sleeve across her dirt-smudged face, realizing she was probably making a bigger mess of it. Her hair was mussed, and wet around her forehead. Long, damp strands had escaped their pins and lay plastered to her face and neck. She sighed, knowing she must look a fright.

She watched Nathan trek down the long row toward her, stirring up dust as he went.

"Garden's coming along real nice."

"Yes, it won't be long now, and we'll be tasting the 'fruit of our labor.' "

His eyes twinkled with humor. "And all this time I thought you were growing vegetables."

Sara managed a weak smile at his joke.

"I wanted to let you know I have an errand in town. I might be late for supper, so don't wait on my account," he said.

"Fine, Nathan." She inspected the leaves of a tomato plant, neatly avoiding his eyes.

"So. . .I'll see you shortly after suppertime," he said as he shifted his weight.

"All right. Bye now."

As he walked away, she wondered if she had imagined the guilt in his voice.

❧

The wagon jolted as a wheel hit a rut on the dry dirt road. Nathan pulled the rig to a stop in front of the Lawtons' house. It was a massive two-story structure on the edge of town. Mr. Lawton owned the new carriage works shop, which, from all appearances, was doing quite well.

He vaulted down and inspected his rear wheels. Sure enough, there was a cracked spoke.

Mr. Lawton came out onto the porch just then and extended a hand to Nathan. "Evening, Nathan. How are you?"

"Evening, sir. Well, I'm fine, but I'm afraid my wagon isn't. I hit a rut and cracked a spoke."

"Lucky for you, I own the carriage works! I'll have William take it over there when he gets home."

Mr. Lawton was a proud man, and Nathan knew he looked upon this as returning a favor for Nathan's help. "That'll be fine, Mr. Lawton. Do you reckon it'll take long to fix? Sara's expecting me shortly after supper."

"Well, Frank will have to get the rest of his work done first. Can't be giving certain customers preferential treatment. Bad for business, you know!"

Mara, who was playing the piano in the front room, stopped to greet Nathan as they passed. She would have gone on and on, but Mr. Lawton cut her short, saying they had work to do. He guided them up the stairs and showed Nathan the room where the water closet was to be.

"Here's the supplies I ordered," Mr. Lawton said. "Finest available. Letitia can't wait to get this installed. Been pestering me about it for weeks."

Nathan took stock of the supplies. Everything seemed to be there. When he'd offered to help with the task, he hadn't realized they were thinking of the second story. He'd helped Pop install theirs, but it was on the ground floor. This would take more time that he'd allotted, but since his wagon needed repairs, he had nothing else to do. He had offered to help Mr. Lawton in a Christian effort to befriend him. He and his wife hadn't attended church since they'd moved to town some months back, and Nathan was hoping a show of friendship would make them feel more welcome.

He was almost half finished when William came in. Mr. Lawton, who had spent more time watching Nathan than helping, addressed him. "William, I need you to run an errand."

"Aw, Father, I just got home!"

"Now, none of that! I need you to take Mr. McClain's wagon over to the shop. Tell Frank to get to it when he can, but it needs to be finished tonight."

"All right." He shuffled away, displeasure evident even in his walk.

Mara peeked around the corner. "How's it coming, Father?"

"Just fine, princess! Your music sounds lovely on that piano. I could listen to you play all day! Isn't she talented, Nathan?"

"Oh, yeah, you play real fine, Mara."

Her cheeks flushed with pleasure. "That's such a sweet thing to say, Nathan. I'd love to play for you all night, but I'm afraid Mrs. Franklin is expecting me soon. She wants my advice on some gowns she's having made."

"You certainly have an aptitude for that sort of thing. Do have mercy with Mr. Franklin's wallet, though! The last gowns you had made set me back a fortune!" Mr. Lawton said.

They talked awhile longer. Nathan continued to work, hoping Mara would forget about him, but she continued to draw him into the conversation.

William returned with bad news. "Frank says it'll be a while before he can get to Mr. McClain's wheel. Says he'll have it done by midnight."

"All right, son."

William sauntered off, and Nathan addressed Mr. Lawton. "I'm not sure what to do. Sara will be expecting me shortly, and I don't want her to worry."

Mara cut in with enthusiasm. "I'll drop by and let her know! Mrs. Franklin lives out that direction. Why, it's practically right on the way!"

Nathan was skeptical about this plan, for he didn't think Sara would want Mara dropping by for any reason. Mara must have noticed his hesitation.

"I insist! It won't be any trouble at all!"

"All right, then. Thank you." At least Sara wouldn't worry.

Mara flew out the door, her petticoats swishing behind her. Mr. Lawton laughed and boasted about his generous daughter.

At last the water closet was finished, and Mrs. Lawton insisted he stay for a late supper. They ate on fine china around a smooth, varnished table. He hadn't spent much time with Mrs. Lawton, but that night he saw many similarities between mother and daughter.

Wanting to be gone by the time Mara returned, he said his good-byes and walked out into the warm, humid air. He was tempted to walk home, but he had left his rifle at the house and didn't want to be supper for a hungry wildcat.

It was going on 8:00, too late to call on neighbors. But then he remembered that Reverend Hill was a night owl, and Nathan knew he would be welcome there. So he set off with new purpose to the little cottage on the other end of town.

☙

Sara glanced at the mantle clock for the fifth time in ten minutes. It wasn't even 8:00 yet, but it seemed much later. Never had time dragged so slowly!

Her feet were folded under her as she sat on the settee, working halfheartedly on her needlepoint. She'd taken a bath after supper—as much to pass the time as to remove the garden grime—and now she sat in her pristine white nightgown, long damp curls cascading down her back.

Nathan is with Mara right now. She struggled to think of something else, but her mind kept returning to this crushing reality. She wondered where they were, what they were doing at that moment. Her eyes burned as her imagination ran rampant. She wasn't completely naive about the ways between a man and woman. True, her knowledge was vague and untried, but she knew the stirrings she'd felt when Nathan had kissed her. The very thought of him causing another woman to feel that way. . . ! There was a burning in her stomach, like fiery coals.

She set aside the material and lay down on the cushion, as tears rolled down her face and soaked into the soft fabric. She remained there, curled up in a ball, until sleep came, like oblivion, finally delivering her from her cruel thoughts.

The striking of the clock startled Sara awake. She was disoriented at first, unaccustomed to waking up on the settee.

Then she remembered.

Turning up the lamp, she peered at the clock as it delivered its final stroke. Twelve o'clock.

Sara's heart dropped. He was not yet home. The terrible fluttering in her stomach grew worse and she feared she would vomit. If only that were all it would take to stop the wrenching pain in her heart.

Nathan. She knew he didn't love her, but he seemed to care for her a little. Didn't he know she'd worry when he didn't come home? Questions filled her mind until they overflowed. Pointless questions, for there were no answers.

This could not go on. She couldn't continue in this manner—loving him—while he unknowingly flayed her soul.

She stood up and paced the floor with nervous energy. She had to confront him, tell him she knew everything. Confess her love for him. It would be painful to admit her feelings when she knew they were not returned, but it couldn't be worse than this torture she was enduring tonight.

She dried her face with the sleeve of her gown. She would just be honest with him. He couldn't get angry at her for that. And if she lost him? She didn't know she hadn't lost him already. Another woman held his heart, and wasn't that the part she desired above all?

Oh, Father, if You could just cause Nathan to love me!

She stopped in front of the fireplace and stared beyond the hearth into the cold grate. There was a scattering of dead ashes there, but neatly stacked above them was a pile of freshly cut logs, waiting to be ignited.

A thought took root in her mind, and she seized onto it.

God, if You would just send a spark into Nathan's heart and fan it to flame, so that his love would burn for me, as mine does for him!

The familiar clattering of a wagon drew her eyes to the door. She stood there in the middle of the room, fixed, waiting for him to enter. On the outside she was unmoving, but everything within her trembled with dread. She wondered if he would be mussed up from a passionate embrace, and if he would look guilty when he found that she had waited up for him.

Her eyes teared up, but she locked her jaw, determined to see this through to the end.

She heard the doorknob as it turned and saw Nathan's form as he stepped quietly inside and shut the door. He turned and was removing his hat when he saw her.

"Sara!"

The room was dim, with only one lamp lit, but she saw him coming closer.

"What are you doing up? I didn't. . ."

He must have seen the tears in her eyes for he stopped in his tracks. "What's wrong? What happened?" His voice vibrated with tension, and his eyes searched hers, as if he could extract an explanation from them.

Sara swallowed, trying to dislodge the giant lump in her throat. "I–I know where you were tonight," she whispered.

He looked completely caught off guard. "You know where I was tonight. . . ?"

"Yes. I know you saw Mara." A tear escaped and ran a

crooked trail down her face.

"Sara, I did see Mara, but—"

"Please, Nathan! There's something I need to say, and I want you to let me finish."

"All right. Go ahead." His brows furrowed, and he looked for all the world like he didn't know what she was about to say.

She turned to face the heatless fireplace so that he wouldn't see the tears that were beginning to course down her cheeks. "Mara approached me weeks ago and told me about the two of you. Everything. I've known almost all along—about how you asked her to marry you, about her father rejecting your suit, about me being second choice as a wife. . ."

"Sara! That's just—"

"No, Nathan! Let me finish!" She turned to face him, letting him see her anguish. "I know you've been seeing her, even after we married," she whispered. There was no censure in her voice, just raw pain. "The night Mara came here—I was outside when she left. I heard her say she'd see you tonight. I've known all along where you were going tonight. I knew all along it was her you loved, and still. . .still I lost my heart to you. When you didn't come home tonight, I thought my heart would break in two!"

"Oh, Sara. . ." He took a step closer, but she held up a hand to stop him.

Her lip quivered, and she bit down to still it. "I made a decision while I waited for you tonight—it's time I told you how I feel. I love you, Nathan." She rushed ahead. "I know you don't feel the same about me, but if you just give it some time, maybe someday you can find it in your heart to love me." Her eyes pleaded with him, and he closed the distance between them.

He gently took her face in his hands. "Can I speak now?" he asked.

She gave a small nod and lost herself in his intense gaze.

"You don't have to wait for someday, Sara. I love you now."

She tore herself away from his hands. "Don't torment me, Nathan!"

"Look at me, Sara!" It was a command she obeyed. "Everything Mara said—it was a lie! I'll admit she was smitten with me when her family moved here. She was very forward, letting me know she was interested. But I wasn't. I never courted her, or met with her—much less fell in love with her!"

"But tonight. . . What about tonight?"

"Oh, Sara. Tonight I installed a water closet at the Lawtons' house! When you heard her say she'd see me Friday, she was just talking about that. I promised her father months ago that I'd help him."

"You were so late!"

"One of the wagon wheels got a crack in it, and I had to wait until it was fixed. I take it Mara didn't come by and tell you?"

"Mara?"

"Yes. When I realized I would be delayed, I didn't want you to worry. Mara offered to stop by and let you know. Some help she was!" he scoffed. "While I waited for the wagon to be repaired, I visited with Reverend Hill, never knowing you were worrying! I'm sorry, Sara, I should've known what Mara was up to."

"No, Nathan. It's I who am sorry. I should have had more trust in you. . ."

"None of that matters right now. All that matters is that I love you."

"And I love you."

Nathan gathered her tiny frame close for a kiss before sweeping her up in his arms and carrying her up the stairs to his room.

epilogue

October 1887

The walk to town had been more tiring than ever before. In fact, everything seemed to be more tiring lately. Naps in the afternoon had become a habit, and Sara was sure Hetty must suspect what Sara herself was convinced she knew.

The cool autumn air was a welcome change, even though Sara dreaded the coming winter months. For now, she would enjoy the colorful leaves fluttering to the ground and the crunchy carpet they made.

As she approached the house, she saw Nathan disappearing into the stable. Her stop at the post office had yielded a rare letter—to Nathan, from a Mr. VanCleeves. She knew he'd want to open it right away, so she headed to the stable where Nathan stood in the doorway.

"'Afternoon, Sara," he said with a warm smile that crinkled the corners of his eyes.

"Hello! You got a letter!" She extended her arm toward him.

"Hmm. . .wonder what this could—Mr. VanCleeves. . ."

"Who's that?"

"It's the attorney I told you about—the one who drew up my father's will." He removed his worn work gloves and opened the envelope. "I wonder what he could want."

Sara watched as Nathan unfolded the pages and began reading. Suddenly he tore away the top page and looked in shock at the one beneath it.

"What is it? What's wrong?"

"It—it's a letter from my father." He gave her the top page, and she read it.

Dear Mr. McClain,

As per your father's wishes, I am sending this letter on to you six months following your marriage. He wrote it at the same time that he hired me to draw up his will. I hope this letter finds you and your new wife faring well.

Very Sincerely,
Mr. Charles VanCleeves

When she looked up, Nathan was reading the letter from his father. She let him continue undisturbed, knowing the significance of these last words from father to son.

When he finished, he handed the paper to her, then turned away to rest his forearms on the split-rail fence. She turned her attention to the letter, written in the heavy scrawl of an aged man.

My Dearest Son,

If you've gotten this letter, then it means that you chose to marry so that you can keep the ranch. There wasn't much doubt in my mind that you'd do so.

First off, I want to say I'm sorry for any grief my will caused you. Even as I write this, I worry that I'm making a mistake by wheedling you into taking a wife. But I've spent much time on my knees over this, and I know in my heart that God is in it.

Please know that I want so much for you to love and be loved as I was. I don't like leaving you alone in this world with no kinfolk whatsoever. I hope the

*woman you chose to marry will be that special some-
one to you. I'm sure she's a fine woman.*

*Be happy, Son. Serve the Lord, and He will bless
and keep you.*

$$I \; love \; you,$$
$$Pop$$

Sara wiped away the tears that flowed rather easily these
days, and joined Nathan by the rough-hewn fence. Knowing he was overwhelmed, she waited until he was ready to
talk. His hand was warm and calloused under hers as she
stroked it with her long, tapered fingers.

"I was so mad at him when I found out about that will. I
couldn't understand why he'd do that to me—force me to
get married when I was dead set against it." He cocked his
head to enchant her with a tender smile. "And now look at
me. I have a beautiful wife to cherish. Even if you are a
tiny little thing," he joked.

Sara's gaze met his, her eyes twinkling. "Not for long."
She watched as the meaning of her words sank in. His
mouth gaped, and it took two attempts to deliver the
words.

"You mean. . . ?"

Her beaming face was all the answer he needed.

Sara found herself crushed in an embrace, her feet dan-
gling above the ground. He spun her around and in
between his giddy chuckles she heard, "A baby! We're
gonna have a baby!"

Finally, he set her back on her feet, but continued to cra-
dle her against his massive chest. "I'm so happy, Sara. I
wish he could know how happy I am."

Sara tilted her face up to his. "He does, Nathan. I'm sure
he does."